Sex
and
Souls
For Sale

Sex
and
Souls
For Sale

A Chilling Tale
Of Child
Sex Trafficking
In Modern America

A Novel By David B. Watts, Private Investigator

MILL CITY PRESS

Xulon Press
2301 Lucien Way #415
Maitland, FL 32751
407.339.4217
www.xulonpress.com

Paperback ISBN-13: 978-1-66284-408-9
Ebook ISBN-13: 978-1-66284-409-6

AUTHOR'S NOTE

THE NEW JERSEY, New York, and Pennsylvania municipalities and counties, as well as the roads, mentioned in this book are all real, as are some of the various restaurants and other businesses within those locations. The author's purpose is to inject a sense of realism in terms of setting … nothing further is intended nor implied.

Robert Higgins is a real-life New Jersey private detective. He and his wife, Brenda, graciously allowed—no— encouraged the author to include them in this novel. Bob Higgins and the author have collaborated for more than twenty-five years on many real-life investigation cases. We're still at it.

One of the book's protagonists, Claude Frederick "Mack" Mackey, was a real-life person until his untimely passing in 1972. He was not a private detective. He was a quiet, hard-working, loving man who became stepfather to my wife, Linda, until pancreatic cancer took him away. All these years, he has been missed dearly, so the author is honoring his memory by using his name as a lead character. Anyone who knew Mack would approve. So would he.

CHAPTER 1

Mid-afternoon, US Route 1 near the
New Jersey Turnpike, Avenel, New Jersey.

CALEB HASTILY SCANNED his surroundings while fussing with his camera settings and adjusting his position. *I'm zoomed in,* he reasoned. *Gotta stay steady for longer shots.* Taking a deep breath and spreading his legs, he bumped against Angel.

Angel groaned, "Hey, go easy, Cal." She gave way and wriggled several inches to her right. "It's tough enough to be on my belly on this wooden porch for more than an hour, and my muscles ain't used to competing with popped-up nails, either." Frowning back in Caleb's direction, she poked her binoculars through the next set of metal rungs and settled in.

Angel was a griper, always negative. But she went along with whatever crazy scheme Caleb came up with. Finally, he'd come up with one that worked. So far.

Checking his camera focus for the nth time, Caleb whispered, "Let's hope this next asshole comes across quick with the cash."

Under her breath, but intending to be heard, Angel grumbled, "Yeah, not like the last one."

Caleb shot back, "Aw, knock it off. They can't all fall over and play dead. Just keep an eye out, and give me a heads-up if you see anything."

It was an ideal spot. This second-floor porch over a used clothing shop gave a perfect view. Shade from other buildings and two large trees added to their concealment. They had not long to wait. A grey Lexus crept into the parking lot. The driver sat for a moment, his head rotating side to side, studying his surroundings. Balding, fiftyish, and over-weight, he cautiously emerged from his car and, head down, hustled discreetly toward the ground-level front door.

"He's nervous. This is the one, Cal."

"Yeah, he'll do." Caleb's camera clicked three times, capturing his target before its image faded to a blur behind a glass door. As the door swung back, the words "Asian Massage" glistened in the sunlight.

Caleb turned his attention to the Lexus. He snapped off several more shots, making sure the tell-tale massage parlor sign would be visible in the photos, too. Caleb knew his payday depended on solid photographic proof his targets couldn't refute. *No denyin' it, pal. Your car's in the picture, too.*

"Let's hope this one's still married," Angel said cynically. She was referring to their last extortion attempt. Their target had laughed contemptuously and spat into his phone: "Idiot. My wife already caught me. The divorce is final next month … so fuck off!"

"Well, Jelly, my girl," he said, using his nickname for her, "we'll see with this one, won't we?" Caleb grinned, brimming with his usual abundance of self-confidence. Caleb drew back from the porch railing, hunkered onto his left side, and rechecked his settings.

He noted, "We'll get him when he comes out. If we're lucky, one of the girlies will show up too."

Caleb was pleased with himself. *This is a great scam. It's worked so far, and the payoffs have been good. The key is not to get greedy. Make demands they can handle without havin' to dig too deep. Hey, wouldn't some married guy rather pay a few hundred bucks for these prints than call the cops? Or how 'bout soccer-mom wifie learning hubby was making Asian massage visitations?* That last image merited a subdued giggle.

Angel rolled onto her right side and studied her man. Caleb was thin, just slightly over five-nine, with reddish hair and a prominent mole on his left cheek. She sighed. *Ain't nothin' special about ya, baby. Just a plain guy. A little scruffy around the edges, but I love ya, anyway.*

Caleb's support getting her through her "tough days," as she called them, was all Angel needed to know about her man. When he found her on the street, all skin and bones and over-dosed on meth, Caleb took her in. He nurtured her through a rehab program that saved her life.

Unlike those in his circle of loser-friends, Caleb hated drugs. He never forgot what alcohol and pills did to his mother when his father abandoned them. He vowed to stay sober and clean, no matter what. So Caleb did for Angel what he was too young to do for his mother. For her part, Angel put her life in Caleb's hands. They grew closer. As her recovery progressed, she began taking care of herself. She gained weight and started looking good. Caleb was taken aback by Angel's striking appearance. She's become a beautiful woman. *How could I be so lucky?*

Caleb's ego also relished her dependence on him. He enjoyed his role as savior and protector—in contrast to his childhood feelings of helplessness when it came to helping his mother.

Angel was content to follow Caleb's lead, but there were times she felt the need to protect him from himself. She gently

SEX AND SOULS FOR SALE

tried to influence his decisions, but her guarded prodding seldom worked.

While awaiting their next target, Angel rolled back onto her stomach and said, "Ya know, Cal, this is really dirty stuff we're into. You wouldn't like it pulled on you."

"No, I wouldn't," he answered impatiently, "but this time, I'm in charge, and these no-good, cheating assholes are taking care of me!"

Caleb harbored overwhelming animosity toward family abandonment. This scam fed into his need to inflict pain and embarrassment on those he despised. "Cheaters and weaklings … just like my old man," he grumbled bitterly.

He turned to Angel with a worried look. "Hey, you ain't gettin' cold feet are ya?"

"No, honey," she replied defensively. "I'm with ya all the way." He reached over, tweaked her left breast, and winked. "You know, Jelly, I couldn't do it without ya."

"I know, Cal." But she knew better. Caleb had strength. The strength she lacked. He oozed confidence, and maybe he was a little too cocky, but she reckoned her life would be a disaster without him … and probably a lot shorter. She looked upon him as her knight in shining armor, but she wasn't kidding herself. She would often remind herself, *His armor might not be that shiny, but whatever Caleb is into is better than where I was. Life on the street* ... She shuddered.

In chauvinistic-male circles, Angel was considered "a knock-out." At just over five-seven with sandy blonde hair, her hour-glass figure and natural beauty turned heads when she walked past. All of Caleb's friends envied him. Angel, however, was self-loathing and could never allow herself a single positive thought. Caleb never asked about—and she never volunteered—the seedier details of her former life. She and Caleb had each other, and that was enough for both.

Her daydreaming interrupted, she warned, "Here comes another one, Cal. Get ready."

Back on his elbows, Caleb brought the camera to bear and began fine-tuning its focus ring. But a sudden movement in Caleb's peripheral vision captured his attention. He turned to his left and drew back. *Too close. A black sneaker? What the—*

A hard-glancing blow smashed against the side of his head. He puzzled at the loud clank it made. His head hurt like hell. He pulled in his neck and shoulders, expecting a second blow. Scooping the camera up under his chest, and with acute presence of mind, he instinctively removed its memory card. Bewildered, he heard Jelly scream and felt her nails dig into his right arm before a sharp yank took her away. He started to rise. His lungs sucked in air in preparation to fight back. Then a second jarring jolt came ... harder this time. Intense pain overtook Caleb's being as he descended deeper and deeper, faster and faster, tumbling through a spinning, blackening vortex. He fought nausea. *This isn't happening! I must ... ah, I must ... I ...*

CHAPTER 2

Mackey Investigation Agency, Route 22,

Greenbook, New Jersey, 10:45 am.

BALANCING THE SUPPLIES his secretary needed, Mack maneuvered his office door behind him with a foot-nudge.

He shouted, "Nezzie, I'm back. Has Bob Higgins called yet?"

Mack's secretary, Inez "Nezzie" Martin, coordinated files, conducted online research, and juggled clients in the office, allowing Mack and Bob—whom she referred to as "her boys"—to concentrate on field investigations. At fifty-eight, with severely tweezed eyebrows and bright red lipstick, Nezzie's tough exterior belied her inner warmth. She was mother hen, mama bear, and den mother wrapped up in one. Hardly a secretary, Mack and Bob called her their secret weapon and their "astounding sounding board."

"Yeah, boss," Nezzie answered. "Bob said he'll be in at about four or so." As an afterthought, she threw in, "Something about 'the fish at Round Valley getting uppity.'"

Mack smiled, shook his head, and thought, *Bob Higgins is the only guy I know who can find time to fish, yet keep up with this screwy, demanding business.* "That's great, Nez. And what time did you say that new client is coming in today?"

"He'll be in at four, too. He sounds all shook up. And just so you know," Nezzie waggled her head side to side for emphasis, "he's dead serious about not involving the cops in his problem."

"Uh-huh. Wonder what that's all about?" Mack fingered through the mail on his desk and said, "Oh yeah, please call Penny, and tell her I'll be a little late. If it's okay with her, tell her pizza at Mr. Assante's later, okay?"

"You got it. Is she at the E.R. now?"

"Yeah, until five or so."

Penny and Mack's wedding day was two months off. He was a fifty-two-year-old widower and she a thirty-five-year-old divorcee. Penny, an emergency room nurse at Morristown Hospital, worked rotating shifts. Mack often joshed he was being punished for all the years Margaret had to put up with his wild shift-swings back in his police workdays. That was before cancer brought a tragic close to their lives together three years ago.

Over the course of last year, Mack and Penny became friends, then lovers and soul mates. Penny, formerly a victim of an abusive ex-husband, was a cheery, energetic woman who bubbled over with enthusiasm. She managed to pull Mack out of his slump as he struggled with the loss of Margaret. Mack marveled at Penny's perseverance. She just would not allow him to wallow in misery. He loved her for that, *and ... oh, those freckles.*

Mack thought about his four o'clock meeting and was intrigued. He might just end up sending that potential client away. *No need to get crossways with the police at this point in my life. Still, I've always been a sucker for a good mystery.* He would hear the guy out.

Claude "Mack" Mackey, a New Jersey private investigator for over twenty years, loved his work. While shying away from matrimonial and custody cases, he managed to carve out a niche for himself working for lawyers and businesses in the central New Jersey area.

His friends, Bob and Brenda Higgins, worked together at Skylands Investigations in northern New Jersey. Mack affectionately referred to them as "B&B" and called on them when he needed help on cases. Mack figured this case was one requiring Bob's intuitive input.

Bob and Mack came at investigative challenges and obstacles from different perspectives. Bob would calmly stand back and take in the whole picture before offering his opinion. Mack, more a direct-action type, looked at a problem as something to hit head-on. He thought of himself as a "full speed ahead, damn the torpedoes!" kind of guy. Because he knew himself all too well, Mack appreciated Bob's more thoughtful process. Together, they were a hard-to-beat team.

Both Mack and Bob came out of law enforcement—not unusual for private investigators. Mack started as a Plainfield detective and Union County Prosecutor's Office investigator. Bob Higgins paid his dues as a twenty-year trooper with the New Jersey State Police, retiring as a sergeant. Solid teammates, they often bounced strategy and field tactics off each other: Bob the strategist, Mack the tactician. With Nezzie handling the office phones and online research, this trio made for a series of happy clients.

This next case, though, would be a true test of their skills and forbearance. With far-reaching implications, this case would take them into a domain beyond human decency and comprehension. This next case would take them into the dark underworld of sex trafficking.

Shortly before 4 p.m., Nezzie looked up and took a measure of a young man standing before her. *Hmm. Mid-twenties. Impatient, arrogant, maybe a toughie. He's nervous. Seems tormented,* she thought. *He can't stop fidgeting—back and forth, one foot then the other.* Her first instinct was to pity the kid, especially for the thick, white bandage on his head. After her extra soft and pleasant hello, she said, "You must be Caleb. You called earlier?"

"Yes, ma'am. Is the detective here?" he replied, gazing anxiously around the room.

At that moment, Bob Higgins sauntered in and, with a wink to Nezzie, walked past and into Mack's office. After a moment or two, Nezzie rolled her chair back, leaned through Mack's office door, and announced, "Your four o'clock is here, Mack." She leaned in farther and added in a whisper, "… and he's a mess."

Sharing a blank stare with Bob, Mack said, "Send him in, Nezzie."

Caleb entered hesitantly. With bloodshot eyes and a grim expression, he scanned the room cautiously, taking everything in. He looked from Mack to Bob and back again.

Mack stood and stuck out his hand. "I'm Mack, and this is Bob. We work together." He motioned to Caleb, who gingerly lowered himself into a chair in front of Mack's desk. He looked like he would bolt at any second.

Mack looked down at Nezzie's note on his desk and leaned back. "So … Caleb, your call this morning has my interest. I'm not sure we can do anything for you yet. But we are good listeners. Oh yeah, by the way, anything you say from here on in stays here."

"Yeah, I got that." He was edgy.

Mack drilled down. "The first thing we have to go over is why you won't report whatever this is to the police." Mack and Bob locked eyes for an instant, thus catching Bob up with that stipulation. "Then I will take down as much information from you as you can come up with." Mack paused and let that sink in.

Caleb squirmed in his chair and said, "Well, I can't let the cops in on this because these guys threatened to kill my Jelly. I mean, her name is Angel. And, uh …" Caleb stalled a moment. His voice grew stronger. He said, "Are you sure this is, whaddya call it … confidential?"

"Absolutely."

"All right," Caleb took a deep breath and continued. "Ya see, Jelly and I were working a scam. A kind of extortion thing. We took pictures of guys going into and out of Asian massage places and then threatened them with exposure if they didn't pay up. Once we followed them home and had their addresses, it was easy to go online and get the rest." As if to partially excuse it, he added, "But we never asked for a lot of money. Just easy enough for them to handle. Like a few hundred. It kind of depended on the car he drove and what he looked like, ya know?"

In near disbelief at such a frank admission so matter-of-factly delivered, Mack and Bob sat staring, stone-faced. Mack spoke softly, "Go on."

"Well, on the last job, I got hit over the head. And when I came to, Jelly was gone. Her binoculars and a broken fingernail were on the boards next to me." Caleb's eyes began to water, as his voice jumped an octave. "I swear, if I ever thought there was any danger in this for her, I never would have—" He lowered his head and sat there, tears flowing, defeated.

"Ahem." Mack cleared his throat. Bob dissolved slowly into the other chair and squirmed uncomfortably.

"So … you're telling us your girlfriend has been abducted. There has to be more—"

His voice rising, the young man interrupted, "Yeah, and it's not about me here. They've got Jelly. She's not a strong person. She was an addict a couple of years ago. It wouldn't take much to—"

Mack interrupted and retrieved a lined pad to make notes. "Okay, okay. Let's start by taking down your contact information and everything about the last time you saw Jelly. What's your full name, cell phone, and home address?"

"Caleb Worten. I live at—"

"Whoa! Did you say 'Worten'?" Mack leaned forward, scrutinized Cal more closely, and almost fell out of his chair. "Cal Worten? The snot-nosed kid Chief Bill Worten and I took pistol shooting about a dozen years ago?"

"Well … yeah. He's my uncle."

"Jesus. What happened to you?" Mack frowned and sat back hard. "When your old man took off, Bill took you under his wing. Then you just up and disappeared."

Caleb looked like he wanted to disappear into the folds of the chair. "I know. That was wrong. I shoulda kept in contact."

"Now I know why you're here," said Mack, nodding in disgust. "You can't go directly to your uncle without involving law enforcement. And you'd have to answer for running out on him, right?

"I suppose you could put it that way, but—"

"No!" Mack stopped him. "You're not pulling any con job here, mister." Mack got up and walked to look out a window overlooking Route 22 traffic. After a few seconds of chewing on his lower lip, he turned to Bob and said, "Watch him." Mack resolutely headed out of the conference room toward his office.

Caleb grabbed his armrests. He spoke up in a panic, "Where are you goin'? Whaddaya gonna do?"

"Whaddaya think I'm gonna do? I'm calling Bill Worten right now."

"Please. Don't!" Caleb shouted. "You said this was confidential."

Mack took several steps back and pointed at Caleb. "Let me tell you something, junior. You can't run out on everyone like your old man did and waltz back in with a personal problem expecting everybody to jump. And jump according to your rules, for Chrissake. Besides, loyalty trumps confidentiality around here. My friendship with Bill Worten goes back too far to disregard over a little twit like you!" Mack was steamed, and he wasn't holding back.

To bring the temperature down a notch, Bob Higgins finally chimed in. He calmly posed, "Mack, I think there's a way around this."

Mack made a sour face.

Bob the peacemaker continued, "I know, I know. But haven't we worked with Chief Worten off-the-cuff before? I bet after he gets over the initial shock, he'll figure out a way to work with us. That gives the kid the space he needs and gives us the hook into law enforcement we would need in this case. Whaddaya think, huh?" To emphasize, Bob tilted his head and gave that "Hey, why not?" look.

His eyes narrowing, Mack shot another disgusted look at Caleb and sat back down. Bob let Mack simmer for a couple of moments, then sunk the hook. "We gotta think of the missing girl too. Maybe we can dig up enough—soon enough—to give the feds a leg-up if we can't find her ourselves. After all, this is a kidnapping case. The FBI will be interested."

Mack relented. "Okay, okay, I get it. I'll call Bill and see what he says." Mack gave Caleb a dark look and said, "I can't wait to see his reaction when I tell him you're involved. You're lucky your uncle is a decent man. Let's hope, for your sake, that he doesn't throw you to the mercy of the justice system. For now, we need to work on getting Angel back." Mack added wistfully, "That is if she's still alive."

With that, all three sat in silence for a long moment. "Okay?" Mack waved a small tape recorder at Caleb, who consented by nodding his head. "Nezzie, the lady you met on your way in, will transcribe this for future use." Mack settled back in his chair, pressed record, and said, "Okay, Caleb, let's have it all."

Further debriefing pried out as much as Caleb could remember at that point. Mack and Bob found it disturbing. Especially the part where Caleb explained, "That night, after I got stitched up in the emergency room, I got a phone call. He said if I didn't produce my camera's memory card, they would kill Angel."

"What could be that important about a memory card?" Mack asked.

"Uh-oh," Bob muttered with raised eyebrows. He rose, perched on the edge of Mack's desk, and leaned forward into Caleb's face. He muttered, "Just what the hell have you gotten yourself into, kid?"

Caleb was flustered. Again, on the verge of tears, he whined, "I know … I mean, I don't know. We were just—"

Mack interrupted and said bitterly, "You were just messing around and stepped into something bigger than you could handle." He picked up his cell phone and punched at its contact list.

Union County Chief of Detectives, William Worten, answered with, "Don't tell me, Mack. Let me guess. You're calling me during dinner because Penny finally wised up and kicked your skinny ass out."

Mack's lack of a smartass comeback was out of character in their relationship. He got right to the point. "Bill, it's personal. It's Caleb. He's back, and he's in a pile of trouble. Can we meet tomorrow? Let's make it somewhere away from your office."

"Shit! That damned kid again."

"We need to talk. It's bigger than him. What time tomorrow?"

CHAPTER 3

615 Clarkson Avenue, Brooklyn, New York.

ANGEL WAS IN complete darkness. A humming furnace and the clanking of steam pipes, along with pungent dampness, told her she was in a basement. She gingerly felt her way around and surmised that she was confined in a small room.

She found a door and banged on it. She hollered at the top of her voice but received only her own echo. She stumbled over a chair, righted it, and sat down, trembling. She felt nauseous. Her head ached. With every exhale came a raspy hollow moan from deep in her throat.

She desperately tried to remember how all this came to be. She recalled being with Caleb on the porch, but everything else was muddled. *Blood ... Cal's head. That rough hand holding a cloth over my face. That strong medicine smell, and a burning sensation. Oh, God!*

More began to flood back: waking up in the back of a van, a visual staccato of lights bombarding her senses. It seemed she was in a tunnel. Angel recalled her head wobbling back and forth in slow-moving city traffic and trying desperately to stay alert. Doing her best to focus, she saw herself looking at a large man seated next to her and remembered turning her attention forward and thinking that something was wrong. There were two of him! She remembered wondering how he could sit next to her in the back seat and be driving too. *I was drugged. That must be why I saw two of him.*

She had no idea how long she had been captive. Hours, maybe a full day had gone by since she was taken. Angel shielded her eyes when, with no warning, a ceiling light came on. A woman's voice said, "I have some food for you. Eat."

Angel cried out, "Why am I here? Who are you? Stop. Don't leave me!"

It was over in seconds … the woman was gone. Between choking tears, Angel gobbled down a McDonald's burger and drained a coke.

With the light left on, she was better able to take stock of her situation. A porta potty in a corner and a mattress leaning against one wall suggested this room was set up for more than a few hours' stay. She slowly approached a dirty wall mirror and wet-thumbed a circle in its center. A stranger looked back at her. *That can't be me. What's happening?* Her hair was tangled, her face drawn and tear-streaked, and her skin had a pale, sickly look.

She shrugged one shoulder and said matter-of-factly, "I can't do this." She shuddered and sank into a dismal state, wailing piti- fully, her arms clutched across her breasts, and rocked side-to- side in the chair. She sobbed, "I'm not strong. I need my Caleb!"

"How is the new one doing, Annika?" Arkady spoke through the Bluetooth in his Mercedes S-Class as he glided smoothly along the Whitestone Expressway.

"Hard to say, brother. She is still a little woozy from the chlo- roform, and she cries a lot."

The younger brother offered, "She's very pretty. If you work on her, she could bring us a nice return."

"I am already on it. I lit the room and she's eating. I will have her under control and willing to cooperate soon. She's weak, impressionable."

"Good. Have the twins returned yet?"

Annika said, "No, and I haven't heard from them. Maybe they are having trouble finding the kid's apartment."

"No, that shouldn't be a problem. Ilia knows his way around New Brunswick. As soon as they call in, let me know. We need that memory card. By the way, my meeting at Brighton Beach went well. I'll be home soon."

Siblings Arkady and Annika Stasevich were born in Brooklyn to Russian immigrants. The elder Staseviches escaped Belarus in 1994 after Alexander Lukashenko was elected by disposing of his opponents the old-fashioned way. They simply disappeared in the night.

As members of the resistance to Lukashenko's authoritarianism, Mikhail and Nadia Stasevich had to run for their lives. They settled in Brooklyn, and soon their daughter, Annika, was born, followed the next year by a son, Arkady.

Mikhail Stasevich had been a professional craftsman back home in Belarus. His small, intricate carvings and costume jewelry caught on quickly in the Big Apple. The children grew up in a law-abiding home with parents grateful to be free of totalitarianism.

Unfortunately, the young siblings fell in with a group of hardened street criminals, who, as was usually the case, preyed upon their fellow neighborhood immigrants.

Two particularly violent members of the group were the Borisov twins, Vadim and Ilia. What they lacked in finesse, they made up for in muscle. Both were imposing: six-four, and each weighing in around two-seventy. Arkady and Annika made good use of the twins. When reason failed to work on shop owners foolish enough to resist or even protest protection money payoffs, the twins "flexed their muscles" … problem solved. The mere physical presence of the Borisov twins also assured personal safety for the more diminutive Annika and Arkady.

The twins, though controlled by Arkady and Annika, also carried out "special contracts" for other mobsters when outside help was needed—a kind of lend/lease arrangement.

What raised Annika and Arkady out of their old neighborhood and to a new level was their discovery of human trafficking. One night, after a bout with vodka, one of Arkady's pals took him to a brothel in Queens. Afterward, Arkady asked, "Where do these young girls come from?"

What he learned and took home to his sister opened a whole new lucrative, criminal enterprise for them. From that point on, with the help of the Borisov twins, they moved in on the human trafficking trade and soon were making international contacts. Graduating from low-level street crime, this brother/sister team was advancing up the criminal ladder. And their growing reputation was not lost on a certain Russian mobster in Brighton Beach.

At first, they tricked illegal immigrants with promises of citizenship and working permits, only to imprison them until they could be shipped off to operators of slave camps in third-world countries or into the sex trade. Women and children of either sex were fodder for their business activities. However, they discovered a lucrative niche right here in America. Preadolescent children from South America were in demand ... especially among wealthy upper-class professionals. Moreover, when taken from their homeland and distributed promptly, these children posed little or no risk to their abusers.

Being part of the distribution chain was one thing, but the real money was in stealing them and selling them yourself. "That's 100 percent profit with no middleman," Arkady would boast.

The young entrepreneurs were smart enough not to infringe on the New York Korean mob—well known in criminal circles for their sex trafficking—so they asked permission to enter the game on their own. The Koreans agreed; however, there were caveats. The siblings had to kick back a percentage to Jopok, as the Korean mafia was known, and to stay away from Greely Square. That neighborhood was "owned" by the Koreans. And the young duo was supposed to spy on the Mott Street Chinese gang for Jopok whenever the opportunity arose.

24

That last part troubled Annika, the more thoughtful of the pair. She said, "We're playing a dangerous game, Arkady. One misstep, and one side or the other will come down on us hard."

"I know, I know, sister. But the opportunity is too great to dismiss. When you went to NYU and studied economics, didn't you learn that those who take risks succeed, and those who don't die on the vine?"

"It's not that I am averse to risk, my brother. I just want to ensure we don't find our necks hanging from that vine. Let's move thoughtfully."

Arkady smirked, "I agree, dear sister, as we pile up a mountain of money."

This was what and who Arkady and Annika Stasevich were: sex traffickers. And they had Angel.

CHAPTER 4

The next day. Elizabeth, New Jersey.

MACK AND CHIEF Bill Worten met at a small luncheonette two blocks from the Union County Courthouse. Chief Worten, the senior-most law enforcement officer in the county, was known as a no-nonsense kind of guy. He had come up through the ranks the hard way. His large and solidly built stature and tough-guy reputation made him an imposing individual by anyone's standard.

Worten opened the conversation with, "So, my friend, what has my nephew done that I should give two shits about at this point?"

Mack gave the chief of detectives the short version and then he went personal. "Bill, Caleb has had a tough time since your brother took off on him and his mom. I know you had a hard time with him too. You did your best to make it up to him, but the best of intentions doesn't always produce the desired effect.

I think this recent incident has jerked him up by his short hair. He's in deep. He needs our help … and so does a young girl named Angel."

"Mack, he is my no-good brother's no-good kid. He was only fourteen when I took him in. He stole money out of my wallet. He picked up with a bunch of local punks and was arrested three times for shoplifting. He was lucky to get juvie probation from liberal judges. God knows what he's been into since." Worten's anger increased. "I tell you, Mack, Caleb is no good—just like my brother. That apple didn't fall far from the tree." Worten shook his head. "No, I want nothing to do with Caleb!"

"I understand, pal." Mack paused and took a sip of coffee. "At least hear me out on this."

Worten sat back in his chair, folded his arms defensively, and said with a sour face, "I'm listening."

Mack leaned forward and spoke in earnest. "Bill, when Margaret lost her battle with cancer, I blamed myself for the longest time. I thought I let her down. But the truth is, there was nothing anyone could've done to change that outcome. Still, I went into a tailspin. For two years I was miserable. It seemed to me my life would be empty from then on out. I was so damned sure of it. Then Penny came along, and everything changed. The sun came out. The happiness I had given up on came back into

27

my life. I tell you from my heart, my friend, we never know how things work out until they do. There's truth to 'it ain't over 'till it's over.' This young man is hurting. If ever there was a time to help him get his act together, it's now. I think he's redeemable. And together, we can do it."

Mack reached into his coat pocket and put a photograph of a pretty young girl down in front of Worten. "This is Angel. She was taken. We don't know yet who has her ... or even if she's still alive, but she is Caleb's girl and they both need our help."

With that, Mack's cell phone buzzed. Mack held one finger up, indicating a pause while Nezzie spoke, leaving Chief Worten staring at Angel's picture.

"Mack, you ain't gonna believe this. Caleb is here in the office, and he's frantic. When he got home, he found his apartment a total wreck. Someone tore it apart. I guess they were lookin' for something. What should we do?"

"Sit tight. Lock up, and don't answer the door. Caleb might've been followed back to you. And call Bob Higgins to come down and stay with you until I get back."

Mack pocketed his phone and said, "Well, Bill, things are heating up. Somebody just tossed Caleb's apartment. This means he has something that somebody wants badly. That somebody might just be somebody who you and I'd be interested in."

Mack stopped talking. He sat back, narrowed his eyes, and tilted his head as he stared intently at his friend. Chief Worten held out for a moment. He reacted with a slow exhale and bitter expression, conceding defeat.

"You always were a damned pain in the ass, Mackey. Okay, whaddya want from me?"

"I don't know yet. Right now, I gotta get back to the office. I'll let you know." Mack rose and said warmly, "Thanks, pal. You're a hard nut and a pain in the ass too. That's what always made us a good team."

CHAPTER 5

BY THE TIME Mack returned to his office, Bob Higgins and Nezzie had everything under control. Bob moved Caleb's minivan to a remote spot behind the building while Nezzie monitored the security cameras covering the immediate parking lot and hallways.

Seated around the conference room table, all three stared at an obviously distressed Caleb.

Breaking the uncomfortable silence, Caleb blurted out, "I don't get it. All I had on it was pics of my marks goin' in and out of those places." Caleb searched everyone's faces. "It's not like it was somebody important, right?"

Bob moved to the window, looking out onto Route 22 traffic. He said, "Well, there's something on that card that's important enough to nearly kill you, kidnap Angel, and rip up your apartment. The question is, what?" He turned back to Caleb with a look that could drill into concrete.

"Yeah," Mack agreed. "And until we find out what it is, we aren't getting anywhere with this case. Nezzie, could you transfer those photos onto your computer? Maybe we can catch something Caleb snapped unintentionally—something worth a lot to some bad guys."

"Can do, boss. Give me a few minutes." Nezzie stuck her palm-up hand out to Caleb and waggled her fingers. "Give it here, kiddo."

Squirming uncomfortably, Caleb murmured "Sure, no prob," and handed over the memory card.

Mack spotted Bob in deep thought, staring out the window. He said, "So what's on your mind, Bob?"

"There's nothing obvious here." Bob turned toward Mack. "Caleb doesn't know what photos he took that were out of the ordinary, right? What he calls ordinary, that is."

"Right. So?"

"So maybe the bad guys don't know what's on the photos either. Maybe they just don't like someone poking around in their business taking pictures."

Mack nodded. "Yeah. And maybe they think Caleb stumbled onto something, or somebody, or even someplace. Maybe they don't want to take a chance that he will figure it out."

Bob went on, "Anyway, there are some things we do know." Glancing at Caleb's head, he said, "First, they can be violent. Second, they're not bashful when it comes to federal crimes, like kidnapping. And third, since this appears to be linked directly to those Asian massage joints, we're gonna be dealing with some seriously organized folks."

Mack agreed. "You're probably right on all three points." He turned to Caleb and instructed, "You will be going over those photos with Nezzie and Bob, and you will describe everything you know about each one. Where the photos were taken, contacts made and how, results and attitudes of your victims, and more. Got it?"

"Okay. I can do that. They're all time and date encoded … at least on that card. There is another one—an older one—that we did when we started."

Mack had a pained look. "You mean there's more?"

"Yeah. Well, in the beginning, I didn't think dating and timing were that important. But I learned it was important to my marks, so I did it on the second card."

Bob and Mack shared an exasperated look. Mack exhaled through ballooned cheeks.

"Let me guess," said Bob sarcastically. "You lost the first one."

Smugly Caleb declared, "Nah, it's in the trunk of my van. Wait … I'll go down and get it."

"Oh no, you won't!" Bob ordered. "I still have your keys. You sit right there."

Bob slipped down the rear staircase and out into the parking lot. He looked around as he approached Caleb's mini-van and popped the rear hatch.

From within a van, a football field length away to the east, Ilia remarked, "Vadim. Look. That must the P.I."

His twin answered, "Uh-huh. Let's stay here a while and see what shakes."

They settled down in the van positioned behind the paint store three shops down from Mack's office and waited.

CHAPTER 6

THE BASEMENT DOOR slammed against the wall as her captors flung it open without warning. Her self-pitying reverie interrupted, Angel lurched forward, nearly falling off her chair. She struggled to sharpen her focus. She stood and demanded, "Why am I here? Let me go right now! You have no right—"

Annika Stasevich cut her off. "No. Here, you have no right, little sister. And you might as well get used to it. Sit down!" She leaned against the door frame as Arkady brushed past her. Angel reached back for the chair, but before she could comply, Arkady grabbed her arm and jerked her upright.

"What is your name?" he demanded, pulling her close.

"Stop, you're hurting me!" she cried, trying to wriggle loose.

"Tell me your name!"

Angel thought fast, enlisting the name of her best friend in high school. "My name is Judy. Judy Wycoff."

Arkady smirked. He gazed down at the floor, turned his head toward his sister, and sighed.

Annika read from a small notebook. "Angela Esposito, also known as Angel. Born August 17, 1995, in Elizabeth, New Jersey. Parents: Stefano and Adriana Esposito, immigrants from Lombardy, Italy. She is single with no siblings. Though first in her class, she dropped out of Rutgers University's child studies program after her third year."

Annika paused and peered over the top of her reading glasses. Continuing with a cynical expression, she said, "That same year, 2016, she was arrested for possession of illegal drugs and sentenced to thirty days in Union County Jail." She lowered the notebook and said, "Shall I go on?"

Angel's jaw dropped. "How did you—"

"We do our homework, Angel. And soon it will be time for you to do yours." She softened her approach. "But first, how would you like to get out of this damp basement? How would you like a shower, clean clothes, and better food?"

Defeated and off-balance, all Angel could do was slowly nod her head in submission.

Arkady held Angel close as he hustled her past Annika. He whispered in her ear, "And you're also going to tell us all about that little photo safari game you and your boyfriend have been playing." He winked back at Annika, who was following closely behind.

Half-walking, half-dragged, Angel went along the hallway toward the stairs. At the mention of Caleb, she said, "Caleb. Is he all right? His head was bleeding. I have to know."

"Caleb? Well, it won't be long before you get to see him. Yeah, he's alive. He must have a hard head, from what I hear." Arkady was relishing his power trip.

While Angel showered, Annika and Arkady stood nearby. Arkady commented, "You see, sister? I told you Gregory would be a worthwhile investment. His information will prove invaluable."

"Yes, he seems to have passed his first test. He prefers you call him 'lieutenant,' you know."

Arkady's contempt was evident. He answered, "Idiot! Considering his position in the police department, that's the last thing he should want."

Bob Higgins stood at the rear of Caleb's minivan with the hatch open. He rooted around, and on the left side, he found a man's sock with the second memory card in it, right where Caleb said it would be. As he turned to go back inside, he spotted a grey van parked three stores away. Careful not to visibly react, Bob continued into Mack's building with his head down. Once upstairs, he tossed his head toward the east and said to Mack, "Three stores down that-a-way there's a van parked in the back. It doesn't look right, Mack."

"How so?"

"I don't think it was there two hours ago when I put Caleb's wheels back there. And I don't like the way it's parked."

"Go on."

Bob explained, "Well, it's on the same angle somebody might use to set up surveillance on this place. That angle blocks the driveway to any incoming or outgoing traffic too. It's just out of place. And wouldn't that business be closed now?"

Up until now, Caleb had been attentive and respectful to the back-and-forth between Mack and Bob, but he couldn't hide the skepticism that showed on his face.

Picking up on Caleb's expression, Mack said, "Listen, puppy, this man has more than thirty years of experience picking up on cars and people who just don't look right. It's called instinct, and it takes years to develop. Don't sell it short."

"So what are you going to do?" Caleb challenged, having momentarily rekindled his cocky attitude.

Bob said, "Let's slow down and think a minute. If they followed you here and are actually out there in that van, they're probably waiting for you to leave so they can grab you and the memory card." Bob paused and let that sink in. He continued, "We know they tossed your apartment and didn't get anything, right?"

"Yeah ... so?"

"Do you really want to take the chance they're not out there waiting?"

Caleb blinked several times. He had no comeback.

Bob turned to Mack with a plan. "I suppose we could go out there and roust them, but we'd be better off if the cops did it for us, no?

Mack's face lit up. "Perfect. That way, they won't know you spotted them. They'd assume a patrol picked up on them."

Mack grabbed his cell phone and punched in a number. He grinned at Bob, waiting for an answer at the other end. When it came, he said, "Hey, Phil. Mack here."

"Hello, Mr. Mackey. What can I do for you? Painting your office?"

"I'm a little concerned about your place. Are you aware there is a van parked in the back? I never saw it there before, and at this time of night, well ... you know?" Mack paused, then said,

"I thought I would give you a buzz, because, you know, there have been break-ins up and down Route 22 lately." Mack, now grinning widely, shot a glance at Bob. Bob slowly nodded.

"Jeez, thanks, Mack. I'll go back down and check on it," Phil replied gratefully.

"Uh ... no!" Mack sat up straight. "I think it'd be better if you were to let the local police check it out. Ya never know."

"Uh-huh. You're probably right. Will do, thanks, Mack."

A police scanner resting on the van's console between Vadim and Ilia abruptly came to life. "Unit 22-10, take an alarm."

"22-10 '-kay"

"22-10, check out a van behind Phil's Paints up on the highway. Store owner called concerned."

"10-4 from Greenbrook and Warrenville Roads."

"22-11 backing up."

"Roger, 22-10 and 11, your time is 18:25."

Vadim started the van and cruised slowly out onto Route 22, westbound. The twins shook their heads in disgust as they drove off.

CHAPTER 7

THE BORISOV TWINS stood at Arkady's desk, heads bowed, hands folded, and eyes fixed on the plush oriental rug. His frustration growing, Arkady paced back and forth, angrily yanking and pushing at his office chair.

"First, you didn't bring the photographer along with you. Instead, you grabbed the camera—without its memory card—and the girl. To beat all, you nearly killed the guy, which could bring down heat we don't need. Next, you tore up the photographer's apartment without consulting me. You even made a threatening phone call to try to clean up your bumbling mess. Then, to top it off, you did surveillance on a private investigator's office and nearly got caught by the police. Why do you think we give you limited assignments with strict instructions? You are not supposed to think. You are supposed to do what we say. Understand?" Arkady's punch swung the chair completely around.

Vadim, the more talkative of the two, rationalized, "We were just trying to protect you. When we saw the two of them taking pictures, it just seemed the right thing to do. For all we knew, they got the client's picture too. We had to react, Arkady. It just got out of hand when we tried to make things right on our own."

Ilia smirked and pitched in, "Besides, you did end up with another good-looking girl, right?"

Arkady strode up to Ilia and finger-punched the huge twin on the chest several times. "You still don't get it. It's not your decision. You should have watched them, called me, and taken down their license plate number. This wasn't a time for you to be thinking with your muscles. Do you understand? As for the girl, since when do you decide who we pick up? There is research that goes into every capture. This is way above your thick heads. Lucky for you, she isn't someone important."

Towering over Arkady, Ilia submissively nodded his head and was joined by his twin.

"Now, get out of here while I try to clean this up."

Annika strolled into Arkady's office as the twins retreated. She said, "Well, they don't look too happy. Another ass chewin'?"

Arkady loosened his tie and straightened his chair. He said, "You know I love those guys. Without them, we wouldn't be

41

where we are—although I'd never let them know it. But sometimes they get in over their heads. They drive me nuts!"

"I know, brother. You would think between the two of them they would have one functional brain working—twins or not."

"Yeah." Arkady chuckled. "We just have to keep our eyes open and try to anticipate their next mistake."

Returning to the issue at hand, Annika asked, "So, after all their screwing up, how do you propose we handle our missing memory card? We can't just ignore it. There's too much at stake."

"I'll take care of it, but with a little more finesse," Arkady said, fussing at a speck of lint on his sport jacket.

Annika threw a long leg over a side chair and sighed. "Oh, I know you will, my brother."

CHAPTER 8

NEZZIE AND CALEB were deeply into scrutinizing over two hundred prints made from both memory cards. A never-varying pictorial theme emerged of middle-aged men slinking in and out of massage parlors, their body language choreographed by fear and guilt.

Bob appeared with sandwiches and coffee and announced, "Break time. Let's eat."

Caleb whined, "I don't understand what looking at all these photos will prove. They are what they are." He shrugged and bit into his ham and cheese.

Bob and Nezzie started talking at the same time, then stopped. Bob deferred, "Go ahead, Nez."

"Well, sometimes, Caleb, little things jump out at you and make all the difference in solving a case. We have to keep searching and talking about what we are seeing."

Bob acted as if a light bulb went off in his head. He erupted from his seat, exclaiming, "Nezzie, you are a genius! I don't care what Brenda would think, I could give you a big wet kiss!"

Nezzie blushed and drew back. "Whatever are you talking about?"

Bob turned to Caleb, "What we should do is start over and have you narrate each photo. Tell us what happened that day, including your impressions—even those things that didn't seem important at the time. Talk it out. Give us a kind of traveling dialogue that takes us to each place and circumstance. We're gonna relive those moments and see more than those photos alone can show us."

Nezzie raised one tweezed eyebrow and slyly said, "You took the words right out of my mouth, Bob."

Caleb rolled his eyes as Mack came in and announced, "Chief Worten is on board, everyone." He turned to Caleb and said, "You said you got a phone call and they threatened to kill Angel if you didn't turn over the memory card, right?"

"Yeah, and they sounded like they meant it."

"Okay, here's what we're gonna do next. Caleb, you will arrange to have all your cell phone calls shared with this phone number." Mack wrote the number on a slip of paper. "We will set it up so the calls coming into our special office phone will be recorded, and we'll hopefully identify the caller ... or at least, the phone number. We're behind, people, and we need to play catch up."

Bob explained their procedure for reviewing the photos. Mack agreed and said, "Okay, then. Let's get started. Caleb, how many massage joints did you say are involved here?"

Caleb answered, "I didn't say. It was all we could find. I think there should be about thirty or so, but we went to them more than once ... a lot more. So, we could be talking between seventy-five and a hundred stops."

With a sickening look, Mack said, "That's just great." He thought a moment and said, "Nezzie, we're gonna have to bring these places up on the computer, figure out the landlord for each, and check with the New Jersey Secretary of State for company owners and directors. We need to put the pieces of the puzzle together."

"On it, boss."

CHAPTER 9

LIEUTENANT GREGORY MIKELS swung his feet up onto his desk, crossed his legs, and leaned back, intertwining his fingers behind his head. He closed his eyes and saw himself piloting that thirty-eight-foot Regal up Florida's inter-coastal waterway, smiling, and waving to other boaters. He imagined the smell of salt air and felt heat dissipating with the breeze against his face. Just as he turned to smile at his blonde girlfriend in a bikini, the daydream dissolved.

"Lieutenant, we got a squeal. Some woman over on Route 27 claims her apartment was burglarized. Patrol guys are on scene waiting for us."

Receiving no response, the young detective waited an uncomfortable moment. Finally, he repeated, "Lieutenant?"

Mikels cleared his throat and grumbled, "Okay … okay, I'll meet you in the garage." Reaching into his center drawer, Mikels retrieved his Glock 9mm. As he pushed it into his belted holster, his eyes fell upon the tri-fold color pamphlet advertising the used Regal yacht. Mikels sighed and headed for his next assignment. But his mind was elsewhere. *I hope Arkady was satisfied with what I gave him. If I play my cards right, this thing could become profitable. What the hell, helping out an old classmate for a little background info—nothing wrong with that. And for a couple of hundred bucks too.* An image of the Regal boat came back. One hundred fifty thousand dollars! He shook his head and muttered aloud, "Not on my salary, and with alimony payments? Fuhgeddaboudit."

"What was that, Lieutenant?"

"Never mind. Keep your eyes on the road. Come on, move it. Let's get there before supper." Mikels tried concentrating on his work, but that yacht was always there, tantalizing him.

Arkady sat nervously tapping his pen. Russian mobster Yuri Volkov slumped in a side chair before him, staring at the stretched elastic band he rhythmically twirled between his fingers.

Volkov, a powerful and menacing figure among Brighton Beach Russian criminal circles, had a reputation for swift "direct action" when needed. That is, he wasted no time correcting situations and people. A bear of a man in his mid-fifties, Volkov stood just over six feet with a full head of graying hair. He had a prominent forehead and round, Slavic features. But it was his eyes that one noticed right off: dark, intimidating, and piercing.

Never taking his eyes from the elastic band, he said, "You know, Arkady, when we do business together, we share resources. It means we can depend on one another. It's a matter of respect. It's how we expand our reach. It's how we grow." He stopped twirling and glared at Arkady over his glasses. His left eyebrow curled upward when he was perturbed. It was curled.

He said, "Have we not shared special people with you? That Lieutenant of yours should be community property."

Arkady had seen that eyebrow before and the consequences that could follow. He weakly started to offer a response. "I know, but—"

"No, I don't think you do. You and your sister are young and have much to learn. When you compromise a law enforcement officer, you've struck gold. You own him. You also own everything he can bring to you: inside information, good stuff on our competitors, and, most importantly, warnings when trouble is about to come our way. This is a valuable resource, Arkady. You must share him."

"And I will, Yuri. It's just that this is new to him. I have him where I want him, but it will take a little more time before I can say to you that he is a trusted asset. When he realizes we own him … that's when you shall have a share in him."

Relenting somewhat, Volkov said, "I like the 'we' in what you said, and I won't be forgetting it. Understand?"

"Understood, Yuri." Rebuked and relieved, Arkady smiled weakly.

Volkov rose stiffly. "My gout is killing me. Doctor says too much vodka. He's not Russian; he doesn't understand."

"No one understands, Yuri Volkovich."

"One more thing that troubles me, L'vionachik Arkasha,"— referring affectionately to Arkady as a young Russian lion— "is that you have made an agreement of sorts with the Koreans. This could become difficult." Volkov slowly nodded his head as he spoke.

"Yes. As I mentioned at our last meeting, the Koreans insist on a kickback and want to know what the Chinese are up to. My sister has concerns in this area. Frankly, so do I. Any suggestions?"

"Be subtle, and let the Koreans know you and I are friends. That should help keep you safe." Volkov then cautioned, "But even that won't matter if you take too big a bite."

Arkady agreed, "Oh no, Yuri, we know our place in the pecking order."

Abruptly, Volkov rose and headed for the door. He paused and said, "I thank you for loaning us the twins when needed. They are rough around the edges, but they handle last resort jobs very well. But do not forget," he waggled his forefinger at Arkady, "I want some of that Lieutenant too."

Arkady was left staring at his closed office door, thinking, *In time, Yuri Volkovich ... in time.*

"Well now, that went well," said Annika sarcastically upon entering the office. "I was listening on the intercom."

"Better than you think, sister. With Big Daddy Volkov behind us, we're on our way." Arkady rubbed his chin thoughtfully and added, "Let's think something up soon to put Lieutenant Greg deeper in our pockets."

"Okay," Annika answered. "Could that have something to do with getting our hands on a certain memory card?"

Their mutual smirk settled that question.

CHAPTER 10

TO SAY THAT Angel's new room was an improvement over the basement would be a vast understatement. While still small, the room had a twin-sized bed with clean linens, was well lit, and had a pleasant lemon smell. The lack of a window troubled Angel, but she was grateful for what she had. Having eaten and showered, she was feeling more like herself.

She took a moment to assess her situation. *So far, these people haven't hurt me, but what is it they want?* She calmly thought it out. *They took me while Caleb and I were doing our thing at one of the Asian joints, so that must have something to do with it. We must have taken pictures of somebody or something that has them upset.*

With a deep sigh, she said aloud, "I warned Caleb that stuff could get us in trouble."

Obeying previous instructions, she walked down the hall to the bathroom, passing several other doors. She found herself in a long hallway with heavy metal locked entry doors at either end. This place had an institutional look … like an old school or factory. The green paint. Doors with wires built into a thick painted glass on the top half. She knew she'd never be able to get through them to escape. On her way back toward her room, she tentatively checked the other doors, but all were locked.

As she reached the door to her room, she heard a lock keying behind her. One of the heavy doors opened, and a small woman entered the hallway. Her sandals slapped on the tile floor, and, as she approached at a steady pace, Angel could see that she was elderly and Asian.

In a heavily accented and choppy voice, the woman asked, "You Ange?"

"Ye-yes, Angel," she answered. Then, she added defensively, "What do you want?"

The woman firmly took Angel by the elbow and said, "You come."

Angel pulled away. "I'm not going anywhere unless you tell me what's goin' on here."

The woman cocked her head and said softly, "I Rosamie. From Philippines. Seamstress. You come get fitting." Her expressive, nearly toothless smile and a slight relaxation of her grip on Angel's elbow seemed reassuring. Angel was confused, but she complied. The little seamstress nodded her head up and down vigorously, pointing to the opened hallway door.

Angel murmured, "Well, I guess one step forward is better than sitting back there, waiting—and for what?"

Rosamie sandal-slapped ahead of Angel along several corridors. As they reached an intersection, a heavy-set woman ushered a stream of young girls along, some in their early teens ... most were younger. Their young eyes darted about fearfully as they passed. Several faces were tear-streaked. One of the smaller ones stared pleadingly at Angel, then they were gone as quickly as they appeared.

Angel was baffled. She demanded, "Who are they? Where are they going?"

Rosamie said, "New group come, I think." She winked and added, "Learn sex. Make money. Better life, I think."

"What? They're just kids! What are you saying?" A dark and sinister reality was beginning to dawn. Angel's mind was churning—images she tried to deny—but couldn't.

"Hey, stop." She grabbed Rosamie's blouse.

"Tell me ... and I mean now. What am I doing here?"

The little seamstress coyly answered, "Boss lady say you pretty. You special. Bring big money."

Angel drew back in horror. A furious rage rose inside her. It bubbled up from deep within her being and spewed out uncontrollably.

"Like hell!" she bellowed. She pushed the smaller woman against the wall and squeezed her throat. "You take me to the boss lady right now, you twisted fucking pervert, or I swear I'll kill ya." At that moment, Angel was exhilarated. Amazed at herself, she wondered, *Is this really me? I don't know where it's coming from, but I like it.* She squeezed harder.

Rosamie, her eyes bulging, nodded quickly and raised her hands in surrender. Once free of Angel's grip, Rosamie calmly stepped out of her sandals. Her eyes narrowed. In one fluid motion, she grasped Angel's right wrist with both hands and twisted it behind Angel's back, pushing up brutally. With her right foot, she swept Angel sideways, slamming her to the floor, and callously rammed her knee into the small of Angel's back.

Angel, her face hard-pressed and distorted against the floor, screamed, "You little bitch! Let me go. Get off me!" But the pain became too much. Angel relented, pleading, "Okay, okay. Let go … please!"

The little seamstress slowly rose and eased up the pressure on Angel's arm. "If you no good, I hurt you more, I think. Ange unustan?"

Defeated once again, Angel nodded, got up, and limped along ahead of Rosamie. But something had happened. Angel momentarily blotted out the lingering pain in her shoulder. She marveled, *Wow! Was that really me back there? Where did that come from? It felt good!* Though wincing in pain, she managed a smile.

CHAPTER 11

NEZZIE HELD HER hand over the phone's mouthpiece and said, "Mack, it's Chief Worten for you."

Mack broke away from Bob and Caleb going over the down-loaded photographs and answered on speaker. "Hey, Bill. What's up?"

"Mack, I have Special Agent Walt Jenkins on with us. He will explain the FBI's role in our current situation. Jenkins, this is Investigator Mackey, prior law enforcement, a very solid P.I., and a friend."

Agent Jenkins explained that the FBI takes the lead early in cases of abducted children under the age of twelve but doesn't get involved in adult cases unless there is evidence that a state line has been crossed. They do, however, monitor adult cases and offer whatever assistance is required to accommodate state and local authorities.

"I will be here for you, Chief Worten. Whenever you need something that we are uniquely qualified to offer, just call. I will set up a file when I hang up and email you the case number. You are, of course, familiar with our encrypted email system?"

Worten said, "I am."

Agent Jenkins continued, "Mack, since you are a private agency, I'm not permitted to conduct investigations directly with you, as I'm sure you know. But we can be in contact through Chief Worten, if that works."

Mack winked over at Bob and said, "Sounds good. We appreciate your cooperation."

When Agent Jenkins hung up, Chief Worten asked, "So where are we at this point, Mack? Do we know anything more?"

"Not much. We are going over the photos and trying to stir Caleb's memory up a little. I've fixed the phones so all of Caleb's cell calls come through to my special phone line. We'll be able to overhear conversations in real-time, as well as record them automatically." Mack hesitated, then added, "You know, Bill, there is something you can do right away."

"What's that?"

"If I give you a bunch of addresses, could you run them through your intelligence files to see if anything shakes out? You know, like narcotics, fencing stolen property, extortion, and most of all, sex trafficking. They are all Asian massage joints, just so you know."

Worten laughed. "Oh yeah, that should be interesting. You do know those intelligence guys guard their information like grandma's knickers. But don't worry. I'll take care of that part. I'll call in some overdue favors."

As the phone call ended, Mack heard a commotion in the conference room.

Caleb pushed his chair back and cried out, "Stop! Back it up. There … check that closer!"

CHAPTER 12

IT WAS THE end of a twelve-hour duty shift, and Lieutenant Mikels was exhausted: two sexual assaults, a hit-and-run, and a possible murder case. *Too much*, he thought. He took the last of the stairs and sighed deeply as he entered his small third-floor studio flat. He threw his jacket over a chair, grabbed a cold beer from the fridge, and pushed back the heavy drape.

He grumbled sarcastically, "What a view! I'm overlooking the friggin' New Jersey Turnpike during rush hour." He fumed on, "This is not what I've worked for all these years. She takes the house and the kids and leaves me with a pension I can't get for another five years? And here I am living in a goddam shoebox in Linden. I've gotta get outta here somehow."

Two beers later, in the middle of a CARFAX commercial, his cell phone buzzed. Dreading a call from headquarters summoning him back to work, he hesitantly answered, "Yeah?"

"Hello, Greg … uh, Lieutenant. Do you know who this is?"

Mikels sat upright. He blinked a few times, nixed the remote, and composed himself. He thought, *Arkady. Maybe he needs something else.* In his best cop voice, he replied, "Sure. How ya doin?"

"I was hoping we could get together again. Your assistance last time was very helpful. I may have something more if you're interested."

Brooklyn, the next day

Lieutenant Mikels found himself sitting across from Arkady with Annika beside him in an adjoining side chair. The siblings made small talk that included showering praise on Mikels for the personal data he'd given them on Angel. The mood was light. Mikels sat smiling, trying to appear as much at ease as his hosts. But his stomach was churning. He stewed. *What do they want this time? Is it something I can do without risking everything? For Chrissake, let's have it!*

Finally, Arkady got to it. "Lieutenant, there is something we need, and we think you are just the guy to take care of it." He stared at Mikels for a long moment. Arkady's attitude had changed. Pleasantries dismissed; he was all business.

The experienced detective in Mikels picked up on it. *He's changed—more commanding.* He managed a hoarse, "Okay, what are we talking about?"

Arkady said, "Someone has something that could hurt us. It's a camera memory card with embarrassing pictures if you get my drift."

Arkady waited. Annika shifted in her seat in anticipation.

Mikels cleared his throat and squirmed, never quite finding a comfortable position. He frowned. "What kind of pictures?"

"Not your problem. Your job is to get that memory card … no matter what." Arkady stood and walked around to the front of his desk and sat on it, which had the effect of exercising dominance over Mikels.

Mikels recognized the tactic immediately; nonetheless, his concern centered on how far he was willing to go to accommodate his old schoolmate.

Arkady drilled down. "Two of my associates messed up by trying to get tough, but that didn't work. We think you have, shall we say, certain persuasive powers that the average person doesn't." He sat back and casually added, "And there's five grand in it for you."

Before Mikels could react, Arkady leaned forward into Mikels's space. In a tone intended to sweep away any resistance, he said, "C'mon Greg, you've been around. You know the score. What do you say?"

"I … uh, I dunno. I'm willing to go a little over the line, but I'm not into intimidation stuff. Getting ya background info is one thing, but—"

Arkady laid his cards on the table, harshly. He leaned back and confidently said, "Oh, you'll do it, Lieutenant. Because if you don't, we'll leak it to your department that you have been illegally selling police information. And I bet if someone checked, they would find a computer trail leading right up to your report on Angel—which, as we've been saying, you did so well."

With a slight smirk, he concluded, "You'll do it, Gregor, because now you have to."

Mikels turned to Annika as if for help. She sat staring at him, emotionless.

Mikels felt a chill. He tried to reason, "You wouldn't. You couldn't. I would deny it, and … and you would be in trouble too."

"You just don't get it, do you? When you do your police thing, you have a badge that protects you. You're the good guys, right? You are among the so-called 'righteous.' When you work for us, the rules are different, Gregor. There is only one rule. That rule is 'do it, or else.'"

Mikels frowned, drew back indignantly, and erupted. "Hold it now! You're fucking threatening me?"

Annika's low-key, acid voice cut in. "Now you're gettin' it, Gregor." She glanced at Arkady and said caustically, "I knew he'd get it. I told you he was smart."

Mikels' eyes darted from Annika to Arkady and back. Their expressionless faces told him all he needed to know. He was trapped, hopelessly ensnared. His head dropped to his chest with a long, slow exhale. He felt numb. His thoughts were flying a mile a minute. *What the hell have I gotten myself into? If I back away and try to report this, I'll be cooked at headquarters. Goodbye pension. But a glimmer of hope seeped into his thought process. But if I go along with them now, maybe I can figure a way out somewhere down the road.*

Arkady gently patted Mikels on the shoulder. "Don't fret so, Gregor Mikhailovich." He paused and let that name sink in. "Oh yes, my friend ... we found that your grandparents were from a small village just outside Moscow. That would be Rostov Veliky, right? You share our Russian blood. You belong with us now. You will be rewarded well, but only if you do as we say." He winked at Annika and finished with, "It's okay, Gregor. Welcome to your new family."

Mikels stared at the desk, his mind in limbo. Arkady handed him a note with Caleb's address and description, leaving the means and methods up to him. Mikels nodded his head throughout the remaining discussion without comment. He knew he'd been had.

An hour later, as he crossed back into New Jersey, Mikels' apprehension wouldn't ease. He reviewed various scenarios that could play out if he was discovered: horrifying disgrace, loss of his job and pension ... maybe even jail time. Worse, what would his kids think of him? These terrifying thoughts haunted him throughout his drive home.

As Mikels drove somberly—almost in a trance—southward on U.S. Route 1, a boatyard came into view just ahead. Gloom and doom shoved aside, he eased off the gas. There they were: the beauties proudly lined up. Posed alluringly, some were on trailers, some on wooden stands, their smooth, shapely bows angled to face the highway. Beckoning. No, more like summoning him. He braked hard and thought, *What the hell—no harm in lookin'.* Suddenly relieved of agonizing distress, he felt uplifted, exhilarated. He smiled wickedly at himself in the rearview mirror and said, "Gregor Mikhailovich, why don't you stop and take a look at some pretty boats?"

CHAPTER 13

"WHAT'S GOIN' ON in here?" Mack asked upon entering the conference room.

At the computer, Nezzie spoke over her shoulder. "Caleb's onto something. He thinks we found the right set of photos."

Caleb frowned at the screen and slowly said, "I'm pretty sure this is what we're looking for. I just need a minute to think."

Bob Higgins signaled Mack with a raised index finger that said, "Give the kid some time."

The group fell silent for a moment. Then Caleb spoke, quietly, hesitantly. "This place was a little strange ... I mean the layout. It was bigger than the others. I remember I couldn't get the guy's car in the picture without movin' around. Ya see, we were set up in my minivan ... umm ... across the highway. I was, like, able to put him and the massage sign together, but I couldn't do it with his car. I had to move over a couple of parking spaces. After we moved, I saw a car down a lane, almost behind the building. I didn't pay attention to it at the time." He paused and stared at the screen. "Go forward one or two, Nezzie, please."

Nezzie clicked the mouse.

"Stop. Stop right there. See? On the far right side, there's the car … actually, it's a van. I was concentrating on getting what I wanted, not on anything else, so—"

Mack cut in. "Nezzie, can you enlarge that part on the right?"

"Sure, Mack."

Before anyone else could react, Caleb pointed and yelled, "There! I bet that's the bastard that clobbered me. See the black sneakers?"

Mack caught something else. "He's stepping from the side of the van and holding onto something. It's small. Looks like … like, maybe a doll … no, it's a child's arm."

Bob added, "Yeah, and another guy is coming around the side. Wait … closer, Nezzie."

The clarity diminished as Nezzie zoomed in as far as she could, but it was good enough. She asked, "What is a child doing at a place like that?"

Ignoring Nezzie's question, Bob leaned in close to the screen and said with astonishment, "Damn! Those two guys look a lot alike. Are they twins? And that is a little kid's arm!"

Mack exclaimed, "Jesus, Caleb! What you two stumbled into looks like a sex trafficking ring, and these guys were delivering a kid to that address."

Bob chimed in, "Uh-huh. And you got made. Either they spotted you or someone connected with them saw your setup—probably when you moved your vehicle—and they ratted you out. All they had to do was alert their other operations and watch for you to show up next time. When you did, they jumped on you and Angel."

Mack instructed Nezzie to print 8x10s of that and several other photos. When she finished, she covered her face with her hands and shuddered. The concept of a small child being delivered to a sex operation was more than she could handle.

Bob said, "Let's put together what we have. It looks like a set of adult male twins grabbed Angel and clobbered Caleb for inadvertently stumbling into their operation. They grabbed Caleb's camera, not knowing he'd removed the memory card. They think these photos could be a threat to them, so they're keeping Angel as bait to get the memory card back." He looked to Mack for more thoughts.

Mack tilted his head. "Yeah, but it's not that simple. I don't see them trading Angel for the memory card." He turned to Caleb. "You two know too much. Suppose after you got Angel back you would decide to go to the cops? No, I think they want to get you and the card. Then get rid of you."

"You mean … kill me?" Caleb was incredulous. "Are you kidding me?"

Mack doubled down, "No, we're giving it to you straight. These guys don't play fair. Hell, they don't play at all. There's too much money involved in sex trafficking to take a chance on you."

Bob added, "And human life is the least of their concerns. That is, unless it turns a profit."

Nezzie murmured a disquieting question. "So is that their plan for Angel? Turning a profit?"

With heads down, no one could look directly at Caleb for a long moment. But Caleb's reaction was immediate. He shouted bitterly, "I'll kill every last one of them if they do that. I swear!"

"Take it easy, kid," Mack said. "First, we don't know if that's their plan. Second, they're sure to contact you again, which is why we set the phones up, right?"

Caleb answered, "Yeah, I suppose." But his anguish wasn't eased.

Mack went on, "Maybe we can smoke 'em out by giving them the older memory card in exchange for Angel. At the very least, it's a way to figure out their intentions about a trade. If they try to double-cross us, we still hold the memory card that counts, and we can continue our investigation."

Bob agreed, "Uh-huh. That will give us the time we need. We might even be able to follow them from the meet. Ya never know."

Nezzie, sympathetic to Caleb's despair, took his hand and said, "Don't worry. My boys will get her back."

With his eyes fixed on the floor, Caleb softly said, "I hope you're right."

CHAPTER 14

CALEB PARKED HIS minivan in his usual spot. As he headed for his first-floor apartment door, he heard footsteps behind him. He sped up. The footsteps kept pace. Caleb stopped abruptly. He suppressed his fear and spun around to confront his follower. Parking lot lights were behind the stranger, so Caleb could not make out his face, but he could tell the man in front of him was tall and well-dressed. Caleb belligerently demanded, "Who the hell are you, and what do you want?"

"Calm down. I can be a friend … or not. It's up to you," said the stranger in a subdued voice.

"This is about Angel, right?"

"Uh-huh." Getting to the point, the stranger said, "It's not complicated. A simple trade: the girl for the memory card."

"How do I know—"

The stranger interrupted, "Oh, stop with that. Think about it. What other choice do you have? You want her back, and we want the memory card. It's simple." He jutted his head forward and said, "Do the right thing."

Caleb said, "I need to know Angel is okay. I won't do it without seeing her first."

"Look, you need to know I work for serious people. These are people who get what they want, one way or another. By the way, they express regret for their clumsy first attempt. But don't mistake an apology for weakness. I'm here to make it right and to make it happen."

Reminded of his injury, Caleb reflexively rubbed the top of his head. He took a couple of breaths, slowly nodded, and said, "Okay. How do we do it?"

"I assume you don't have the card on you right now."

"No. I only look stupid. But I can get it fast enough."

"Okay, here's how it'll work." He handed Caleb a disposable phone and said, "Keep this charged and on you. I'll call you and give you instructions when the time's right."

Caleb persisted. "When will I see Angel and know she's okay?"

The stranger shook his head and answered, "Listen, this is on our schedule, not yours. You do as we say, and you'll get her back. And one more thing. Leave those P.I.s out of this."

Caleb blinked several times, feigning surprise.

"Oh yeah, we know you've been to their office in Greenbrook. You want her back safe? Leave them out of it. You will do as you are told if you want to see Angel again."

Caleb glumly nodded his head in surrender. The stranger made a dismissive gesture, indicating Caleb should go inside, and walked away.

Bob Higgins sat in the rear of his van 200 feet from Caleb's apartment in an adjoining lot. Speaking into his two-way Motorola radio, he said, "Okay, Mack. He's leaving and heading back to his Ford. He's looking over his shoulder, making sure Caleb's not following him. He's looking all around too. You were right; he's too sharp to tail. Plan B comin' up."

Mack replied, "Okay, Bob. Remember, all we want is his plate number, so when I pull in wide in front of him, make sure you're on his tail so you can get it."

"No sweat. He's comin' at you with his lights off."

Caleb's stranger warily drove along the row of parked cars and turned toward an exit onto Easton Avenue. Just as he arrived at the edge of the road, Mack swerved wide and nearly side-swiped him. Lurching to a skidding stop, Mack lowered his window and began cursing.

"What the fuck are you doing, you stupid shit? Put your god-damn lights on! Where'd you get your license?" He flipped the bird and drove on into the lot.

It all took place in seconds. Bob came up behind and took down the stranger's plate number. All three drivers then went their separate ways.

Mack and Bob waited fifteen minutes in a gas station half a mile away, then met back at Caleb's apartment to review what had just happened.

Caleb opened the door and remarked, "You're too late. A guy was already here and threatened me." Caleb followed Mack and Bob into the kitchen area, continuing to harangue them. "If you had gotten here a half hour earlier, you would have caught him. Some detectives you guys are!"

Bob gave Caleb a dirty look and passed a paper to Mack. "Here's the plate number—it's a cream-colored Ford Focus."

Caleb blinked several times and sat down at the kitchen table. He whispered, "Sorry. I didn't know you were around. I guess you do know what you're doin'."

Mack said, "We wanted you to act natural, so we didn't tell you."

"So why didn't you grab him? Maybe you coulda gotten him to tell us where Angel is."

"It doesn't work that way in the real world, Caleb. He might not even know where she is. He's only a messenger."

Caleb asked impatiently, "Well then, what's next?"

Mack said, "We test them. You give over the old memory card, and we'll see if they give Angel up. I doubt they will, but it's worth a try."

Caleb wasn't convinced. "But what if they know the difference between the cards? What if they figure out we have more, including the one we think is important—the one with the van and the twins in the driveway? What would they do to Angel if we don't play straight with 'em?"

Bob explained, "First, this plan will confirm for us that that's the card they want. They'll also know we aren't chumps, and they should play ball with us." Bob paused and flashed Mack a glance. He went on in a more apologetic tone, "Caleb, don't count on them giving up Angel easily. She's valuable to them in more ways than one."

Caleb caught Bob's meaning. His head dropped into his hands, and he moaned, "Please, stop saying that. Not my Jelly."

Mack went to the wall phone next to the fridge and called Chief Worten for a lookup on the cream-colored Ford Focus.

Worten called Mack's cell phone the next morning and reported the request came back "confidential." That is, it could not be revealed without sufficient predication, which Worten didn't have in this instance.

"Bill, that can't be. Bob's sure he got it right. He was up against the guy's bumper. I've never known Bob to get a plate number wrong."

Chief Worten thought a moment and said, "That can only mean this guy has special status. Maybe the government or—"

Disgusted, Mack cut in, "—or a dirty cop."

"Uh-huh, and we need to find that sonovabitch."

CHAPTER 15

ANGEL WALKED WITH Rosamie along several corridors and down two flights of stairs. After their earlier altercation, their conversation was limited to Rosamie's hand-gesturing guidance. Rosamie's no-nonsense demeanor signaled she was also on guard for any further attacks from Angel. But there was no need for concern. Angel had become compliant. She went along, accepting violence would not work against Rosamie. That, however, did not mean Angel wasn't paying attention. Her eyes scanned right and left. She tried to keep track of where they were in the building but found it impossible. She had no known starting place from which to orient herself. She now realized that her earlier observations were correct. The building was an old city-type elementary or high school. The green two-tone paint, the tile floors, and fifties-style light fixtures suspended at intervals along the halls left no doubt. When they passed an open door to what had been the gymnasium Angel caught a glimpse of the children she'd seen earlier. She slowed, but Rosamie gave her a "move on" shove. In that instant, Angel was able to see the children sitting on the floor with the heavy-set woman speaking to them. Angel seethed at seeing them again. She wanted to beat the crap out of Rosamie and do the same to the fatso back in the gym. She wanted to charge in and get those little kids and lead them out of this place. But she remained controlled. She told herself to bide her time. *I gotta stay alert. Wait ... I never think like this. Something is happening to me. I don't know what's coming, but it can't be any worse than what I've been through before.* She caught herself smiling again.

Rosamie caught it too—and frowned. Angel narrowed her eyes and stared at her captor. Gone was that erstwhile fearful expression. This was the face of defiance. A face that said, "I am not helpless. I no longer fear you!"

Without warning, Rosamie pushed her into a small office off the hallway. Just as suddenly, large, vise-like hands clamped down on each of Angel's arms as she was propelled into a chair and held down. Annika stood above Angel, looking down arrogantly with hands on her hips. The twins stood above, leering at Angel as they held her down.

"I hear you learned of Rosamie's martial arts talent the hard way, Angela. Just so you don't get any foolish ideas in the future, you should know that our little Pacific flower holds black belts in both Kuntao and Dumog. She was a Filipina women's champion in the eighties … long before she joined us."

As she spoke, Annika reached over to a small table and retrieved something shiny, which she waved around in her right hand. Angela identified it immediately and began to struggle.

Annika held up the syringe and snapped a middle finger against it. She droned on, "You see, dearie, you belong to us now."

Angel screamed, "No! You will not drug me! I cannot go there again."

She arched her back and kicked. She tried to bite. Every fiber of her body exploded in rage. But the twins were too strong. Each held an arm and a leg down while Annika smacked and flicked at Angel's left inner arm, looking for a vein. Finding an adequately swelled vessel, she eased the needle in and plunged the drug into Angel's unwilling body.

"There now, you just relax and enjoy your Special K. We have a little job for you in a couple of hours." Annika lightly patted Angela's cheek. Giggling, she said, "You are a special present for a special friend, so Special K is quite apropos."

Angel's jaw was clenched so tight she thought her teeth would crack. She continued to struggle. She recognized "Special K:" Ketamine, the date rape drug. Hopeless! She locked eyes with Annika and screamed venomously, "Before this is over, I will fucking kill you!"

Annika laughed haughtily. "Before this is over, as you say, you will be long gone in more ways than one."

Angel's eyes rolled back. Time slowed. In no particular hurry, several seconds flowed past while a familiar, warm, soothing curtain enveloped her. Fading gradually, irreversibly, into a place she knew all too well, her last thoughts struggled to form. *When I come back from this terrible place, I will be stronger. I will win! I will* ... Time stopped. Angel dissolved. She felt herself liquefy and flow over the edge into an abyss of nothingness.

Annika remarked coldly, "Hmph, she went down quickly. Looks like controlling her will be a snap."

Turning to Rosamie, she briskly ordered, "Get moving. I want her dressed and ready to go before it wears off." She thought she might have to give Angel another hit before getting her to the beach.

The little Filipina bowed subserviently and purred, "Yes, missie. Which dress best? Red low-cut or white you-see-through?" She put in her own opinion. "White best, I think."

"I don't care ... just make it quick. We don't keep the Russian bear waiting."

CHAPTER 16

———————————————

Caleb's apartment, New Brunswick.

CALEB ANSWERED THE throw-away cell phone with, "All I want to know is whether Angel is okay."

Mikels answered, "She is. You'll get to see her soon. Do you have what I want?"

"I do." Caleb did his best to seem cooperative.

"Good. I want you to drive south on Route 287, then north on Route 1. Stay in the right lane, and go exactly the speed limit— no more, no less. When I think the time is right, I will pull up next to you and signal for you to follow me. Understood?"

Caleb was impatient. "Okay, okay, but when do we do this?"

"We do it right now. I'll be watching your every move, so don't even think about checking in with the cops."

That brought Caleb back to a discussion he'd had at Mack's office the night before. When Mack handed over the old memory card, he told Caleb to do whatever he was told. He instructed Caleb to keep whining about when he could see Angel and make her captors believe he is desperate and will do anything to get her back. Mack also told Caleb not to expect to see Angel quite yet. He was sure whoever had Angel would want to check the memory card before giving her up.

Caleb had protested, "I don't get it. Why are we doing this if we know they won't give her up?"

Mack explained, "We need to buy time. Identifying this guy—your go-between—is crucial. Since we can't do it with a plate lookup, we must try something else. Bob Higgins is working on it. Just go along, Caleb. Just go along for now. You'll see."

"Will you guys be around, like when he came at me that night at my apartment?"

"No, Caleb, not this time. For reasons you don't need to know, we think he is a bad cop. He'd probably pick up on us right away."

Never lacking a smart-aleck comeback, Caleb said, "A cop! So I'll have police protection, huh?"

"Never mind, wise ass. When he calls, just get it done, and call me as soon as you are free of him."

As instructed, Caleb drove south on Interstate 287 to its intersection with US 1 and began driving north, adhering strictly to the speed limit. He reached into his pocket and fingered the memory card, thinking, *Maybe Mack's wrong. Maybe I'll get my Jelly back today.*

Caleb noted traffic was heavy, but no more than usual for this time of day. *He probably wants to blend in until he makes his move.* Caleb closely watched his speed as he drove under the Garden State Parkway, past Woodbridge Center on his right, and crossed over Route 35. Coming up on East Grand Avenue in Linden, a cream-colored Ford Focus cut in behind him and blew its horn. Caleb tentatively raised his hand to acknowledge.

The driver came up on Caleb's left and moved in front. He signaled a right turn and went onto South Stiles Street. Caleb followed. The Ford came to a stop in a remote area behind the Linden Hampton Inn.

Mikels got out and walked over to Caleb's driver door. He said, "Angel is in the hotel lobby waiting for you." He put his hand out and demanded, "Now, let's have it."

Caleb pushed open his driver's door hard, which shoved Mikel's back several feet. Caleb tossed the memory card to Mikels and ran toward the Hampton Inn rear entrance. Over his shoulder, he yelled, "If she's not here, you're dead meat!"

Mikels drove away, thinking that was the easiest five grand he'd ever made.

Sitting crestfallen in a chaise lounge in the Hampton Inn's center courtyard, Caleb dialed Mack's cell phone. Waiting for an answer, he scanned the atrium and regarded employees and guests going about their everyday business. He thought, *My Jelly is somewhere out there, and the world still goes around. God knows what they've done to her, and I can't do anything about it—not yet.* He wasn't used to feeling helpless. He also wasn't one to easily admit he was wrong about anything. But new circumstances presented new lessons. He was beginning to catch on.

"You were right, Mack," he said quietly into his phone. "I got screwed. I'm sittin' here at the Linden Hampton Inn with my hand on my ass and no Jelly."

Mack said, "Okay. Linden, huh? Is there anything else you can tell me?"

"Well, let me think. The guy was average build, taller than me—maybe five-eleven. About forty, dark hair, and he had a thin mustache. I'm sure it was the same guy as the other night. I didn't see his face then, but I recognized his voice. Oh yeah, and it was the same Ford Focus. It has some damage to its right rear fender, just so you know."

"You did great, kid. I'll let Bob know. Now, get back here as quick as you can. Your ass is goin' on ice."

Mack hung up and called Bob Higgins. "It's Linden."

"I'm on it." Bob spun around on Route 22 and headed east.

Mikels drove directly to New York City. He walked in unannounced and, with a triumphant flourish, dropped the camera's memory card on Arkady's desk. "There ya go! The punk was a pushover."

Arkady smiled and scooped up the card. Nodding slowly, he said, "Very good, Gregor. We'll make a Cossack out of you yet."

Smirking widely, Mikels eased into a side chair, expecting further conversation.

But Arkady's attention fell back to the papers on his desk. He nonchalantly said, "Annika will pay you on the way out."

Mikels blinked a couple of times and stared straight ahead. He felt slighted. He got up to leave. Bitter at being summarily dismissed, he slowly walked out and down the hall. *It's a mistake to treat me this way. You'll see. I can deliver much more ... then you'll show me some respect.*

Annika popped out of her office and interrupted his brooding. "I overheard. Wait here."

A moment later, she returned from her office with a broad smile and handed him a thick envelope saying, "Good work, *Lieutenant.*"

Mikels detected a smidge of sarcasm—an unnecessary emphasis of the word. He understood her tone to mean that although he may have been a police lieutenant—an important title elsewhere—that title didn't hold much value around there. That is, other than what you can do for them.

Annika turned and headed for Arkady's office. Mikels, having been sent away dismissively twice, started for the door. Ten steps down the hall, he stopped and whipped around. *Wait a goddam minute here. I won't be treated like an office boy. You people need to wise up!*

At a determined pace, he headed back toward Arkady's office. As he drew near, he overheard the siblings in conversation.

"You know, my brother, this will be a large relief for the senator."

"Yeah, that's true. But the best part is that Brighton Beach hasn't heard of this mess and won't."

"Amen to that, brother! Volkov would eat us for lunch."

Mikels stopped short. What the hell? He silently withdrew. As he approached his car, he chuckled aloud, "Well now, didn't I just hear something above my paygrade? Hmph, a senator. U.S. or state? I wonder which state? And who is this Volkov they're afraid of? I'll just tuck this away and keep it for a rainy day."

Once in the Holland Tunnel, he squeezed the envelope. It was thick. *Let's see, five thousand is fifty hundreds, right? Right.* As the thunder of other vehicles reverberated against the tunnel's sides, he rolled down his window and shouted, "Hey, out there, you thirty-eight-foot Regal yacht, get ready. Gregor Mikhailovich is comin' for ya!"

CHAPTER 17

Two days later, Linden Police Headquarters

LIEUTENANT GREG MIKELS reported for his evening shift. He parked his Ford Focus in the restricted section of the Linden Police parking garage and electronically carded into the building. He greeted the duty desk sergeant with a smile as he passed by.

Sergeant DiGiorno said, "Hey, Greg. Chief wants to see you ASAP."

"Thanks, Tony. I'm on it."

As he rode the elevator to the second floor, Mikels speculated, *Chief probably wants me to schedule more coverage at the high school for tomorrow's protest.* He knocked and casually walked into the boss's office. Seeing no one, he turned toward the small adjoining conference room where Chief Collins often conducted private meetings.

Chief Andy Collins sat at the head of the table, tapping a pen impatiently. "Come in, Lieutenant Mikels." He made no eye contact with Mikels, and his tone was anything but cordial.

When Mikels crossed the threshold and saw the others, his heart skipped a beat. Chief Collins, on the other hand, wasn't in a heartbeat-skipping mood. He brusquely motioned for his lieutenant to sit. Taken completely off-guard, Mikels obediently crash-landed into the only empty chair at the table.

Collins said, "I think you already know Chief of County Detectives Bill Worten."

"Of course." Mikels nodded, nervously acknowledging Worten.

Chief Collins continued, "I want to introduce you to private detectives Mackey and Higgins. But I understand you already know their client, Caleb Worten. Am I right?"

Caleb couldn't contain himself. His eyes filled with hatred, and he started to rise. Mack yanked him back.

The air went out of Mikels. His shoulders sagged. His eyes closed. Nodding his head slowly, with a sardonic half-smile, he muttered, "Worten, of course. I should've known."

The tightly packed conference room fell into an uncomfortable silence for what seemed interminably longer than just the ten seconds it lasted. To Mikels, it was as if a cloud of cleansing bleach had descended over him, attacking his below-the-surface dirt and grime. He felt naked, exposed, as if he was splayed out on an autopsy table with everyone digging through his guts.

Chief Collins opened the conversation. "Greg, I've known you fifteen years. We joined the department together. We went to each other's weddings. We've grown up together on this job." He slammed his fist hard on the table, triggering a startled jump from everyone. "Before I explode and throw you out a window, tell me—what the fuck is goin' on here?"

"I don't know what to say, Chief. I—"

"Well, you'd better come up with something, and quick. In one minute, Chief Worten will be reading you your Miranda rights, and I will be listing your charges. How 'bout this: police misconduct, terroristic threats, accessory to kidnapping ... and that's just for starters."

Panicking, Mikels' eyes darted around the table from one face to the next. "Okay, okay. I'll lay it all out for you. But I gotta know where I stand first. Hey, put yourself in my position."

He paused and took a deep breath, temporarily at a loss for words. His voice jumping an octave higher, he blurted, "Christ, being a perp is all new to me." He took another deep breath. With his head nervously shaking, he said, "I gotta ask the obvious. What's in it for me?"

This was Chief Worten's turf. He laid it out calmly and slowly. "I'll put it to you straight, Lieutenant. It depends on what you say. If it weren't for Angel still out there, I'd have the cuffs on you by now." Worten let that sink in, then got to the heart of it. "That said, Chief Collins and I have gone over your record. It's a good one." Then, with just the right amount of indignant anger rising, he said, "You stupid dipshit! Didn't you realize you were on a fast track around here? You were a good bet to make chief in a few years. Now you've gone and blown all that away."

"I know, I know," moaned Mikels, "but there has to be something I can do to turn this around." He pushed forward earnestly in his chair. "Listen, my wife and kids left me. I'm living in a shit hole with a stunning view of the turnpike's two southbound lanes. I can barely make alimony and support payments out of my paycheck." His voice turned shrill. "Chief, you can add this to my list of crimes: I've been getting comped eats wherever I can on duty 'cause I can't even afford my fucking groceries."

Mikels's pent-up anger kept gushing out. "I used to have self-respect. I loved this job and this department, but a person can only take so much. I've felt like I've been trying to claw out of a hole that keeps caving in on me."

Chief Collins put a hand up and stopped him. "Haven't you heard of asking for help? The department's psychiatrist is here to help with the same problems you describe."

"Oh great, I can just see it now. 'There goes Lieutenant Mikels, the psycho-patient.' Won't that go over nicely with the men and women I supervise?" He shook his head several times in disgust.

"You'd be surprised how many of your co-workers are in some kind of therapy right now." Chief Collins paused a moment. He tried another tack. "Greg, as far as we know, you haven't hurt anyone. You aren't in so deep that you can't work your way out of this hole. That is, if you really want to."

Mack, feeling the moment was right, offered, "Maybe you can tell us how this began and where it stands at this point."

Mikels started at the beginning. When an old schoolmate, Arkady Stasevich, asked for "a small favor," Greg didn't see any harm in it. Arkady explained all Greg had to do was put together a brief dossier on Caleb and Angela, and there would be a couple hundred in it for him. He was assured it was no big deal— nothing beyond a small favor for a friend. Mikels explained that's how he rationalized it at the time. "It seemed harmless enough, and I desperately needed the cash."

He explained how, after he had delivered on that first assignment, Arkady and his sister revealed their true intentions.

"At that point, I realized they wanted that data for illegal purposes. They sunk the hook and reeled me in. They even got cute and brought my Russian grandparents into the mix, calling me Gregor Mikhailovich." He laughed sarcastically. "How could I be so stupid?" Finally, Mikels went over everything he knew about recent events, including overhearing Arkady and Annika mentioning a senator and Volkov from Brighton Beach.

Chief Worten spoke up, "You know, people, there's an old saying: 'There go I, but for the grace of God.'" He was delivering a peace offering of sorts to move toward the ultimate goal of turning Mikels into an asset.

Mikels, now fully into beating himself up, discounted that argument. "Yeah, but I never gave it a second thought once the money showed up. And five grand for the camera chip? That was like a lifeline. I didn't realize I was getting in deeper and deeper. I was climbing out of one hole and burying myself in another." His shoulders bent. Mikels was near tears.

Chief Collins said, "Well, Greg, to use the Staseviches' words, you belong to us now. You will meet with Chief Worten and these two P.I.s and figure out how to get Angel back. If you can make cases against these people, go for it. I'm stayin' out of this for now. You will also work your normal shifts as if nothing has happened."

Chief Collins stood, indicating his participation in the meeting was over. Everyone began to rise. Collins leaned in close to Mikels, and in a threatening, gravel-like voice, he said, "So help me God, you go south again, and I'll burn your ass good!" A second later, he stood up straight and reversed course. In a conciliatory tone, he said, "But if you come through on this, I will also see to it that you get a low-interest loan from the Police and Firemen's Credit Union to help you get by."

Mikels sniffed and whispered, "Thanks, Chief."

Once Chief Collins left the conference room, Mikels collapsed into his chair again. He considered the bind he had gotten himself into. He was faced with the most dangerous and challenging assignment of his career. He would have to work inside and against the Stasevich organization, a fringe element of the Russian mob. Some would consider that a death wish.

Those daunting concerns were interrupted when Bob Higgins said contemptuously, "Okay, *Lieutenant.* Shall we get started?"

Not surprised by Bob's attitude, Mikels looked up and said, "You're not alone, Higgins. My rank has been tossed around negatively in conversation lately by others too. And I do deserve it.

But before we start, I'm curious. How did you identify me? I know you couldn't get a look up on my license plate."

Bob jogged his head toward Mack and said, "He figured you would want to pull off the meeting with Caleb on familiar turf. Once we knew you met at the Hampton Inn here in Linden, we figured you worked for Linden PD—or maybe Rahway, Elizabeth, or some other nearby town. We got lucky when I spotted your Focus in the parking lot right off."

Mikels smirked. "Just good detective work, huh? I thought about borrowing or renting another car, but their license plates could be looked up. Not mine." Mikels shook his head. "Hah! I'm so smart I outsmarted myself."

Bob shrugged.

"Okay, let's get started." Mack kicked off the discussion concerning Caleb's security.

"There's no doubt in my mind that Caleb is at serious risk. They know he has the memory card they want—and that it's been held back. They have no other choice but to believe he would expose them. We also need to identify the subject of Caleb's photo on the day Angel was taken. It's likely someone important. I wouldn't be surprised if it's the senator you mentioned, Greg." Mack looked at Caleb. "We have to get you out of your apartment and to a safe place for a while."

Caleb drew back and said, "You mean I have to go into hiding? Forget it. I need to be in on getting Angel back. I won't do it. I can't just—"

Chief Worten broke in. "Listen to us, Caleb. We can't get Angel back and worry about your safety at the same time. Think about it. We've got Mikels working for us now. He'll be our eyes and ears on the inside. Just what do you think you could do better?"

Caleb stared at Mikels. "Just to be clear, I don't trust you."

Mikels sighed. "Understandable."

Mack looked around the table for support. "He was a bad guy, but only for a short time. It does look like he's come full circle. Anybody disagree?"

Bob reluctantly conceded. "I guess. Let's give him a chance." But he stared hard at Mikels and added, "I'm sure he's considered what would happen to him if he decided to dump us for Ruskie money." Finally, Bob allowed, "Hey, he's the one goin' into the lion's den to get his respect back."

Worten asked, "Anybody got any ideas where we can stash Caleb?"

Mack thought out loud, "I can't see him staying with any of us. That's the first place they'd look. We need a place near enough to keep in touch, yet somewhere they'd never think to look."

Bob offered, "Let me look into that. I have a friend with a place in the Poconos. Maybe he'll work with us. It's less than forty minutes from our house and remote enough that any bad guy out-of-towner would stand out. Nice place. Brenda and I used to go fishing on the lake up there."

It was settled. Bob would set up arrangements for Caleb's security, and they would work with Mikels to find Angel.

CHAPTER 18

BACK IN HER room—or jail cell, as she called it—Angel sat up and threw her bare feet and legs over the side of the bed.

She felt woozy. She remembered struggling with Annika and the twins, but the rest was elusive. Vague, weird notions skipped past and bumped against her consciousness. She remembered someone releasing her from the uncomfortable restrictiveness of clothing. She remembered thinking, *Freedom. Naked. Yay, I'm naked! I feel like a child again. Carefree. Happy.*

But then those pleasant, fantasy-like meanderings became sinister. A man. An older man. Smiling and coming closer. *Touching me. I can't move. I want to move. I must get away from him. I can't! What's happening? No!*

In disjointed segments, it all returned like a bad dream. But it wasn't a dream. She knew what happened.

Still a little unsteady, she gathered herself up and staggered over to the mirror. She took notice of the simple white dress she wore. It was flimsy and diaphanous and had nondescript embroidery along its hemline, more like a nightgown.

"Sheesh. This ain't like no street dress I ever wore." In a matter-of-fact voice, Angel stated the obvious. "I was raped. They drugged me, and I was raped by that old joker." She thought, *Strange, I don't feel a thing. No tears. No shame. Nothing.*

While pacing back and forth, she busied herself with soul-searching. She whispered, "I have a choice. I can fall apart right here. I can become what I was before Caleb came along. It'd be easy to give in and go with the flow. But I'm not goin' there. Not after crawlin' out from underneath that rock once before—and not after seein' what a good life can be. Not gonna happen … not this time."

She picked up the tempo and began walking faster. She took bigger steps. Aggressive steps. "These bastards don't know who they're messin' with. I've been here before. I've lived through date rape and every other kind of evil those degenerates threw at me back then-and I survived. Drugs? No problem. I can mess with them and stay ahead. I ain't the girlie-girlie pansy they think I am. I know these ropes, and the people who have me don't have a clue. You can't survive what I did and not get an education. I'll be one step ahead of them. They don't know it … they're up against a street fighter. God knows, I ain't never been an angel—but this time, this Angel makes the rules!"

Her last thought summoned up a wistful grin, and—even though she was smiling—a tear to go with it. She thought back to the first time she and Caleb dated. He was so patient. She tried to explain she wasn't the girl for him.

She'd said, "You should find yourself a cute little prim and proper future soccer mom. You gotta know, Caleb, that ain't never gonna be me."

She remembered when others referred to her as Angela, right off, Caleb called her Angel. Then she said it and said it strong. "Believe me, I ain't no angel."

Caleb said, "Okay then, let's jump past the first half of this movie and go from there. I know … I'll call you your second half-a-name. You're gonna be 'Jelly' now." He accepted her as she was with no questions. No judging. She thought, *Now it's my turn. It's the least I can do for myself. Yeah … for me!*

In these several moments, Angel's transformation was complete. She would no longer see herself as a victim. With a fisted elbow-pump, her newfound self had to cry out, "Yes!" She relished the moment.

She went to the door and yelled, "Look out, you bastards, there's a new Jelly on the block!"

Seconds later, and with a sudden whoosh, the door swung open, and Annika entered Angel's room.

Irritated, Angel said, "Don't you people ever knock?"

"No, not when it's our door, our room, and our property. Meaning you!"

Angel cried, "You don't own me! No one owns another person. This is America!"

"You have a lot to learn, *Jelly*. And I overheard all your gibberish just now." Annika slowly stalked around the room with her hands authoritatively on her hips. She said, "I came to check on you. What do you remember about last night?"

"I know you drugged me, but I don't remember anything." Angel put her head down and began to sob. "Why are you doing this to me? I am very reactive to drugs. My doctor told me to be very careful with opioids and stuff like that. I'm not a strong person. What did you give me?"

"It was just a sedative to calm you." With that, Annika abruptly started to leave.

Angel whined, "Where are my clothes? Why am I wearing this? It's embarrassing."

On her way out the door, Annika looked over her shoulder, pursed her lips, and said, "Oh, I don't know. It becomes you. Sort of angelic, if you get my drift."

Angel stood there with her shoulders drooping in mock defeat, waiting until Annika's footsteps faded. She suppressed a laugh, thinking, *If they're gonna drug me, let it be smaller amounts. I can handle that and still know what's going on.*

At that same moment, on her way to the first floor, Annika couldn't help giggling at the image of Volkov naked. That fat old fart. It was too bad Angel wasn't with it last night. She'd be laughing today, not crying.

Annika ran into Arkady on the staircase. He asked, "What are you so happy about?"

The ridiculous image of Volkov and Angel together lingering, Annika shook her head and said with a giggle, "You're a man. You wouldn't understand."

CHAPTER 19

HIS TRIP INTO the city whizzed past. Mikels had one of those "How did I drive all this distance without paying attention?" sensations. Melancholy visited briefly when he drove past the boatyard, but he got over it. That yacht business was a fantasy. He realized it had only been a psychological escape hatch from the pressures he'd been under. That stress no longer gnawed at him, but now he was about to become a player in a much more deadly game. This would be more than worrying about his pension or losing his job. *Now I'm screwing with the Russian bear, and no matter how this turns out; he won't like it!*

The Williamsburg Bridge hummed beneath him. He went over the discussion he had with Mack, Bob, and Worten the night before in the Chief's office. Exchanging all the information had been completed and was illuminating to both sides. Mikels was now aware of the second memory card, and the others knew a senator and a Russian mobster were somehow involved. The story was developing, but it had too many loose ends. And how was he supposed to get to Angel? *If I get too pushy, Arkady and Annika will pick up on it. No, I need to be smart. I need to play along and look for a break.*

Arkady looked up from his paperwork and got right to the point. "Sit down. You didn't get what we wanted."

Mikels feigned a frown, sat down, and said, "What are you talking about? I got the memory card, just like you wanted."

Shaking his head vigorously, Arkady said, "It's the wrong one. It doesn't have what we want. You were played."

Mikels was indignant. "Whoa. Just a goddam minute. I did exactly what you wanted, and I did it right. It's not my fault he gave up the wrong one."

Arkady, relenting somewhat, said, "Yeah … that's true. But we're left with the same problem." He stood up and paced. "Not only is there someone important on that card, but our people might also be on it. Someone making the connection could result in big problems for us."

Mikels suppressed a reaction. He wondered if it was the senator that was in the photo. *I gotta get that tidbit to Worten.*

103

Mikels saw an opening. "Well, maybe if you let me in on what's goin' on around here, I can do better when you send me out. How can I get the job done blindfolded?"

Arkady's head jerked up. Surprised, he pointed a threatening finger and said, "You don't tell me—"

Mikels stood up toe to toe with Arkady and cut him off. "Wait! I understand the 'need to know.' I work with that every day on the job. But when important stuff comes up, you don't send an office boy to do a man's work. And that's just the way you've been treating me … like the kid next door who cuts your lawn." Mikels was on a roll. "And while we're at it, that little threat you think you're holding over my head is bullshit. I'm not here 'cause you own me, Arkady. I'm here for the bucks."

Mikels drew his fantasy boat brochure from his jacket and held it out. "Ya see this?" Gazing admiringly at the boat displayed on the front page of the tri-fold, he turned it toward Arkady and said, "This is why I'm here. Money! Yeah. I need you for that, but you need me too. I can get you into where information hides from you. I can let you know when trouble is heading your way too. You need me, Arkady. And I need money. It's a two-way street."

Using his police tough-guy routine, Mikels set his jaw and held his breath, waiting for a reaction.

Overhearing their loud, argumentative voices, Annika joined them. "What's goin' on in here?"

"Our friend Gregor has taken the bull by the horns, sister. He thinks we underestimate his talents. He wants to be in the know." Arkady chewed on his lower lip and sarcastically added, "He's growing balls."

Mikels turned to Annika and said, "I just want it clear. I'm here for the money. I'm not afraid of your petty threat to expose me. It isn't working. What will work is you putting me to proper use … not with half-assed errands anyone can do." He held eye contact until Annika broke away.

"Maybe he has a point, Arkady. He can think … unlike two others we know."

Arkady regarded Mikels suspiciously. He instructed, "Leave us, Gregor. Give us fifteen minutes and come back."

As Mikels strolled along the hall, he waggled his tie and twisted his neck, releasing a trickle of sweat from beneath his collar. He continued down the long hallway of the four-story, mostly deserted school building. The Stasevich office had a sign that said "Spasibo," so named by Annika. Mikels knew it meant "Thank you" in Russian which fitted perfectly with its ersatz role of community outreach to the nearby Russian neighborhood. Of course, Spasibo was a cover for the Staseviches' illegal activities.

Located at 615 Clarkson Avenue in the Williamsburg section of Brooklyn, the school was built in 1922. It closed in 2005, a victim of budget cuts. Owned by the New York City Department of Education, the fine old building was for sale. The likelihood of a buyer stepping up was slim, so Spasibo convinced the board to rent it as a community non-profit.

Mikels observed. The place was huge and probably hadn't been upgraded since the eighties.

He took the opportunity to check further. At the far end of the hall, he found an unlocked door that led to the second floor. Unlike the refurbished first floor, he found paint chipping, stairs worn from decades of treading students, worn doorknobs, and dirty hanging light fixtures. His cough echoed. Despite its decrepit condition, the familiar smell of schoolbooks and reams of paper had faintly survived years of neglect. It brought back memories. Any second, he expected to hear a bell ringing and the clamor of kids carting books from one classroom to another. Checking his watch, he turned to go back down to the office when he stopped short. He thought he heard something. It sounded like a child crying. He waited. Nothing.

At the bottom of the stairs, back in the familiar shelter of the present day, he paused. Looking back up the staircase into another era, he had a creepy feeling. He strained a moment, listening. Again, crickets. *Hmm. I could of sworn I heard ... nah! This place is spooky. It's playing head games with me.*

When Mikels returned, Annika was gone. Arkady was leaning back in his executive chair, waiting for him.

"So we think you're right. You have a certain value—not only to us, but to others too. We will be calling on you, and, for your part, you will be compensated for what you deliver."

"Sounds good. Just one thing, Arkady. You mentioned others, but I don't want anyone else to know who I am. I'll work through you and Annika, but no one else. That not only keeps it simple, but it also maintains security and ensures that I'll be around a while. Now that we're clearing the air, you should know I've been appointed to serve with several confidential units. My chief has me attending intelligence briefings at the county level

... and that kind of thing covers narcotics, terrorism, and trafficking."

Arkady squinted slightly and appreciatively nodded his head. "That's excellent. Anything—and I mean anything—you hear about to happen, even if it doesn't appear to affect us directly, you let me know. It still may have value, understand?"

"Uh-huh. Understood. But again, we need to keep my identity in-house."

"I agree. Leaks happen." Arkady walked from behind his desk and extended his hand. He said, "Gregor, I'm getting to like you. You're ballsy. You might just be on your way to getting that pretty boat."

Throughout the handshake, Mikels smiled through gritted teeth. *Rub it in, you bastard!*

CHAPTER 20

THEY MET BEHIND a cheap motel on St. Georges Avenue in Rahway. Since Chief Worten's black four-door Dodge screamed "detective," he used his wife's minivan.

Worten looked around as he approached Mikels's Ford. The first thing he said was, "Are you sure you weren't followed?"

Mikels ignored the question and, with a sour face, asked, "When you borrowed the wife's van, did you tell her you were meeting an informant?"

Worten settled into the front passenger seat. "This is no time for your prickly humor, Greg. And stop beating yourself up! This isn't all about you, ya know."

"Don't I know it. The more time I spend with these Russians, the more I know they're underworld heavy-hitters."

Dispensing with platitudes, Worten grumbled, "Okay, so talk to me."

Mikels laid it out. "I'm in solid. I have them convinced they can get more out of me than just some computer work at HQ."

"Good. But watch yourself. I don't have to remind you … you can't be directly involved in any criminal activity. Undercover means walking a fine line between believability and becoming as bad as your targets."

"I know. I know. I have Arkady thinking I can warn him when a bust is coming down or when law enforcement has intelligence that would be worthwhile to him. I can avoid involving myself in anything criminal by arguing to protect my usefulness. They have others for direct bad acting. But there are a couple of things I need to pass on to you."

"Shoot."

"First, that photo of the van and the twins at the end of the alley … you need to take another look because the senator is probably the guy Caleb was concentrating on at the time."

"Uh-huh!" Worten was making notes. He stopped and looked up. "I wonder what Caleb did with those photos. I mean … at the time. Did he approach the senator for money?" Back to note-taking, he shook his head and added, "This is one crazy case."

"Uh-huh. Also—and this is a little off the wall—while I was on Spasibo's second floor for a couple of minutes, I could've sworn I heard a kid crying." Mikels grabbed his steering wheel and shifted uncomfortably. "I gotta tell ya, the place is spooky. I'm not sure, but it did sound like a little kid crying."

Chief Worten stiffened. "Now that could be something. Can you take a closer look? If we can be sure kids are being held there—"

"I'll try, but I'm not quite there with these people. So far, to them I'm all talk. I haven't delivered anything worthwhile yet. Just promises. I wish there was something we could do to get them to trust me."

Worten shifted around to face Mikels and said, "Hmm, I might be able to do somethin' about that. How about you warn them of an upcoming raid on some massage parlors … maybe in Newark or Staten Island? What would that do to your creds?"

"Oh yeah!" But on second thought, Mikels was doubtful. "I like it. But they would expect proof it was about to happen, right? How would that work?"

Worten considered that for a moment and came up with an idea. "Let's suppose I could convince a couple of police buddies of mine there was drug dealing going on in a couple of massage joints. It wouldn't be my fault if they came up empty, but wouldn't your tip-off give you the creds you're hoping for?"

Mikels stared at Worten for a long moment, then said, "You are one devious sonovabitch, ya know?"

With a glib expression, Worten said, "You don't get to be a chief by playing softball. You'll learn that yourself someday."

Stoically, Mikels answered, "I think I'm learning it right now. But even if there was no raid … let's just suppose they confirmed there was surveillance going on. I would be golden."

"Okay. I'll see what I can do," Worten said.

They sat in silence for a moment. Mikels asked uncomfortably, "Is Caleb still pissed at me?"

"Wouldn't you be?" Worten sighed deeply.

"There's more to my nephew than you know, Greg." Worten filled Mikels in on Caleb's father deserting the family and how he tried to take Caleb under his wing.

Mikels listened intently and said, "I guess everybody's got an ax to grind."

"Yeah, but in Caleb's case, he couldn't forgive and forget. So he took it out on anyone he saw who was like his cheating father who abandoned him. The targets of his extortion scheme filled that need perfectly."

"All of which brings us up to today, Chief."

Worten said, "Okay. Let's do something I usually do with all my, uh—"

"Informants?" Mikels smiled dryly.

"Okay, you said it. We need a signal to let you know to bail out if we know you're in trouble. It's usually a text or phone call. Which do you prefer?"

"A text, I guess. How 'bout you act like a boat salesman and say, 'Greg, I found a Regal in Delaware. Interested?'"

As Worten wrote it down, he frowned. "What the hell is that about?"

With a half-smile, Mikels mused, "It's a dream that turned into a lost cause. You don't need to know, Chief."

CHAPTER 21

Angel's third floor lockup.

ROSAMIE KNOCKED AND slowly pushed on the door enough to peek inside. In a sing-song voice, she said, "Ange, I come for you."

"Well, don't tell me—somebody around here knocks for a change."

"You come. We look at clothes for you." Rosamie smiled to ease the tension between them, considering their last encounter.

Picking up on Rosamie's attitude and seeing an opportunity to gain information, Angel responded with, "Sounds good, little one. I hope you have something better than that dinner napkin I wore last time."

Rosamie nodded her head too many times and laughed. "Yes. That bery small napkin. You make good joke, I think."

As they walked together toward Rosamie's room on the same floor, Angel asked, "Do you think I could visit with the children? I have younger sisters back home, and I know how to calm kids down."

"Oh, no. Missy Annik no like that much, I think. Kids okay up there." She tilted her head upward toward the fourth floor. "Plenty food, clean beds." Rosamie paused, and, in almost a whisper, she said thoughtfully, "Doing pretty good now. Not like before in other country, I think."

Angel picked up on a change in Rosamie's demeanor upon the mention of children. She tried to go deeper. "Rosamie, did you ever have any children?"

Rosamie stopped short and looked up at Angel, torment apparent on her face. She held up three fingers. Her voice got louder. She answered bitterly, "Yes, missy. I have babies. All dead now. Bahala Na Gang take away all babies in village. BNG no good! Kill everybody. Rosamie in next village same day. Bery bad." She hung her head and blinked for an awkward moment.

"I'm so sorry, Rosamie." Angel touched Rosamie's arm.

Regaining her composure, the little seamstress gazed upward again and said, "These babies gonna have good life. Sexy come early but for better life. America people no unestand, I think."

She shrugged away what seemed obvious to her and continued along the hallway.

Angel was able to suppress her disgust. She had learned some valuable information. She knew the children were being held on a floor above, and she had been allowed a brief glimpse into Rosamie's thought process which could be useful later. But she also gained some insight into the twisted mentality behind child sex trafficking. *They make a business of preying on kids from poor countries and make excuses for child sex trafficking by saying they're better off here. It's crazy. Sick!*

Back in her room, Angel began working on a plan. Somehow, she would make contact with the children. She vowed to do whatever it took to get them out of here. No matter what. *No matter what I must do. I can hold on. I know that, but can a bunch of little kids do the same? I don't think so. They need me.*

What Angel hadn't considered until that moment was that she needed the children as much as they needed her. Their captivity and bleak future were in tune with her new-found confidence. It gave her purpose. She didn't know how, but she knew she would get through all this. She began by reconnoitering. With ongoing access to the third floor, she carried her towel and a bar of soap for cover in case she was questioned and quietly left her room. Not surprisingly, the stairway doors to the fourth floor were locked at both ends of the hallway. Angel approached one of the hallway windows and peered through the years of dirt and smudges.

A fire escape. She reasoned, *Schools would have to have fire escapes. I bet if I could open this window, I could go out and upstairs to the fourth floor.* She pushed on the window, but it wouldn't budge. She checked for locks and found two; one at either end of the sash. The one on the left had a screw missing, so she pushed and tugged at it until it loosened. She was able to turn the whole mechanism around enough for the window to free up on the left side. The right side wasn't as forgiving. She pushed and pulled, but all she ended up with was indentations on sore fingers.

Back in her room, she looked around for something rigid enough to use on the window lock. It wasn't until she turned over her bed that she found it. With a little coaxing, she managed to free an eight-inch flat, metal spacer bar that held the springs to the sidebars. Hefting it in her hand, she smiled slyly.

Energized, she returned to the hallway window, and in a few minutes, she was able to work the second lock away from its intended position. She pushed upward on the heavy window. It wouldn't move. The only choice she had was to pound on its vertical sides to loosen it. After a moment of considering the noise it would make, she thought, *Hey, I've come this far. What the hell?*

Surprisingly, the window loosened from its seizing after just a couple of healthy thumps on either side. Angel waited. No one came. Slowly, she raised the window. She boosted herself up and wiggled out onto the fire escape. The fresh, cool air surrounded her..

Freedom, she thought. *It smells like freedom.*

She turned around, closed the window, and stood up. Then it hit her.

"I'm out! I'm free!" She looked down the building's steep brick wall and saw that the fire escape extended to about ten feet above the alley floor. *All I have to do is climb down and back to Caleb!* Then she turned and looked up. The fourth floor seemed to coldly sneer back at her. It was decision time. She sat back down and reviewed her options.

If I take off, they'll discover I'm gone soon and probably move the kids by the time I get to the police and convince them to come back here with me. If I stay, maybe I can do something to get these kids out. I can't let them fall into the life I had without doing something. They deserve a chance. She looked up at the cold, ancient fire escape ladder and back down. She'd made up her mind. *Oh no, Jelly-girl, you stay and help the kids. Get going!*

She tried not to look down or over her shoulder. The height seemed astronomical. She told herself it could only be forty-five feet or so from the ground. Nevertheless, she held on to the black metal rungs for dear life. At the fourth floor, she discovered a catwalk leading to all the fourth-floor windows on that side of the building. *Great—no more ladder.*

Very carefully, she made her way along the catwalk on all fours. The first window was a darkened storage area. As she *cautiously* crawled to the second window, she began to hear voices. Young voices. She turned her head sideways and lifted her head just enough for her right eye to take a quick peek. What she saw made her heart skip a beat. She counted twenty-three children, ranging in age from eight or nine up to fifteen or so. They were in small groups, most sitting on beds. Several were watching cartoons on television. The whole group was hushed. Tense. It reminded Angel of cattle on her uncle's farm in upstate New York before they were loaded onto slaughterhouse trucks. She shuddered. Angel pulled back and sat down, her back against the wall. Taking a deep breath, she thought, *What now?* She looked around, taking stock. *First, I need to check these other windows out.*

The next window was so dirty that she couldn't see much at all. She licked her finger and smudged away a small peephole at the lower right of the windowpane. She put her eye up to it and came face to face with the heavy-set woman she'd seen in the gymnasium days before. Shaken, Angel drew back and held her breath.

Nothing happened. *She didn't see me!*

Emboldened, she went back to her peephole and soon realized the woman was concentrating on a laptop computer screen. Just inches from the woman's focus of attention, Angel moved her head back and forth to take in the whole room from different angles. *She sleeps and eats here. She lives with these kids and controls them. I'll have to figure out a way to get around her.*

Angel quietly retreated and paused a moment at the children's window for a second look. She withdrew back down the fire escape and back to her room. Before leaving the fire escape's window, she turned the locks back in place. The screws weren't holding anything, but she figured no one would find that.

She sat on her bed, exhausted. Her recent excursion was exhilarating, but it had expended every bit of her adrenalin. She fell back on her bed and drifted off. Before sleep came, however, she murmured aloud, "Angel is winning."

CHAPTER 22

CALEB WAS BRIMMING with impatience in the back of Bob's van. "Why do we have to go so far away?" he groused. "Chrissake, Pennsylvania might be the next state over, but it might as well be the dark side of the moon."

Bob glanced in his rearview mirror. "I told you to stay down back there. Do it! You need to get outta Dodge. It's for your own good and for the people around you."

Instead of driving up Route 31 to 46 and directly over into Pennsylvania, Bob took a circuitous route through Sussex County, New Jersey, then crossed over the new bridge into Milford, Pennsylvania. Several miles of open terrain before the bridge gave Bob assurance he hadn't been followed.

Once through Milford, Bob jumped onto Interstate 84 west-bound for about thirty minutes, then navigated several back roads to the outskirts of Paupack. Caleb pushed up and peeked out at the countryside passing by.

"Where in hell are we, Bob?"

Bob said, "Pretty soon you're gonna be whining, 'Are we there yet, Daddy?' Do you suppose just for once you could shut up? I'm not doing this for the fun of it. When we arrive, you will be respectful to Mr. Sullivan. Eric and I served on the New Jersey State Police together. He's old, but he's tough. He'll keep you safe if anyone can." Bob shot another look at Caleb in his rear-view mirror. "So just sit back and enjoy the last few minutes of this ride through God's country. You'll see Lake Wallenpaupack soon on your left. Great fishing here … almost as good as Round Valley." He couldn't help smiling at the panicked look on Caleb's city-boy face.

When they arrived at the Sullivan cabin, two huge dogs challenged them. Bob got out and spoke to the animals. "Hey there, Thor." He turned to the other. "Rascal, come see your ole buddy, Bob." The menacing growls turned to whimpers. Tails wagged. Even so, Caleb was reluctant to get out of the van.

Eric Sullivan appeared on the front porch and greeted Bob warmly. Dressed in worn jeans, a flannel shirt, smoking a pipe, and walking with the aid of a cane, retired Trooper Sullivan hardly seemed to qualify as anyone's protector. He pumped Bob's hand saying, "You made it." He turned to the van and said, "So. Where's the human cargo I'm about to harbor?"

Caleb gently slid out of the van with both dogs giving him a good once-over sniffing. As he turned his attention to Eric, Caleb was so obviously fixated on the cane that Eric answered the unspoken question.

"Yeah, I'm somewhat of an invalid, but between the dogs and this, you'll be in good hands." He drew back his jacket, revealing the biggest pistol Caleb had ever seen. "It's a Colt .44. You know, Clint Eastwood's sidearm." Affecting Eastwood's speaking voice, he recited, "'… the most powerful handgun in the world.'"

Bob chuckled, enjoying what he knew was coming.

Eric smiled ear to ear and went on. "Since you seem curious, you might as well know that I lost my kneecap in a gun battle twenty-some years ago on the New Jersey Turnpike. But that doesn't mean I'm helpless." He extended his hand. "You'll be safe here, son."

Bob chimed in with, "What he didn't say, Caleb, is he won that gun battle and two bad guys lost. He might have limited use of a leg, but the rest of him is just as tough as ever."

They went into the cabin, and Caleb was introduced to his small room in the rear, near the kitchen. His sleeping quarters consisted of an old army cot and a green, metal dresser. He was flabbergasted.

"Bob, I can't stay here. This isn't me. What will I do all day?" He looked around. The cabin wasn't spacious—more like warm and cozy. The fireplace stood solemnly at one end, complete with a stuffed bear's head mounted just above. There were other animal trophies affixed to the knotty-pine walls as well. A woodsy odor permeated the place.

Eric winked at Bob and said, "Oh, I'll find things for you to do, Caleb. Being a city boy, you will go away appreciating your visit here. Believe me."

The two old friends left Caleb dismally inspecting his surroundings and sat on the cabin's front porch rocking chairs. Bob appreciated the placid atmosphere. Calm. Unpretentious.

"Beer?" Eric reached for his chair's arms to get up.

"Nah. One leads to more, and I gotta get going. We thank you for this, old buddy. We'll do all we can to keep this secret, but you might have your hands full with this kid. He's headstrong and has a problem with authority, if you know what I mean."

"Like we didn't have that same problem?"

"Yeah, I suppose. Overall, I think he's okay. He has grit. You'll know how to deal with him. I've seen you in action."

"So it looks like my assignment might be more than keeping him alive. You want me to become a camp counselor too?"

"Something like that."

Eric nodded and said, "Okay, Sarge. You always had a subtle way of getting your message across. By the way, I haven't kept up with Mack. How's he doin' since his wife passed?"

"He went through a rough patch, but he's okay now. He's getting married in a couple of months. Nice girl. A nurse." Bob couldn't suppress a chuckle. "She's got freckles. I'll tell him you asked." He rose abruptly. "Well, I gotta go." He yelled toward the cabin, "See ya, Caleb! Listen to this old man, and learn something."

The friends shook hands and parted.

Caleb stood on the front porch, watching his sole link to civilization grow smaller as Bob's van bounced and shimmied down the dirt path. He thought, *My Angel, wherever you are, I wish I could be there with you. I am so sorry about this.* Turning to go back inside, his habitual sarcastic wit crept in: *Oh my God. I'm stuck here in upper Slobovia with no internet or cell signal, sleeping on an old army cot, protected by a has-been Clint Eastwood and his dog team. What could possibly go wrong?*

CHAPTER 23

RECOGNIZING THE CALLER, Arkady answered his desk phone quickly. "Yes, Senator, good to hear from you."

New York State Senator Maxwell Sturbridge was normally an impatient man. But recent events had him on the edge of hysteria. With an election just three months off, he desperately needed to have this problem behind him

"Arkady, you know how sensitive this is. We must clean it up immediately. If those photos get out to the public, I'll be ruined. Bad enough that the massage parlor was in the shot, but the, uh—you know."

"Yes, I know. We are doing everything possible on this end, but there have been complications. It looks like the one who took the photos has an idea that there's more to them than just a guy and a massage parlor visit. But he hasn't figured out the whole picture. Also, we aren't exactly sure what's in his photos. You never saw them, right?"

"That's right. He came up to me in front of a flower shop and told me he'd destroy the incriminating photos if I forked over three hundred bucks. He must have followed me from uh …" His voice trailed off. "I told him to drop dead. It was more of a gut reaction. Now that I think about it, maybe I should've just paid him off." Pausing a moment, the senator said in a hushed voice, "I don't think he knows I'm a highly respected politician, or he would've demanded more than three hundred … no?"

"Probably so, sir." Arkady's face soured. *Highly respected, my ass!* "And as far as paying him off, you're right. I'm sure that would not have been the end of it."

"I was so careful that day. I went over to Jersey. I used my wife's car instead of my own with the New York courtesy plates and the gold emblem thingy. Your twins made their delivery in the back discreetly. I thought I had everything covered." Senator Sturbridge went quiet for a moment.

Arkady waited until the senator was ready to continue. When he did, Sturbridge's tone was insistent. "Volkov can never hear of this uh … shall we call it a mishap? He knows about me. He tolerates my private preferences, if you know what I mean. But he made it clear to me I should exercise discretion." The senator's voice became shrill, wavering. On the verge of tears, he cried out, "Arkady, what are we going to do?"

"First, Senator, please calm down. I'm sure Volkov will understand. You and he go way back."

"Yes, that's true. We have a long-standing arrangement: he gets favors from me, and I am rewarded. Hey, politics is politics. But should he believe that I am in the midst of a scandal, I wouldn't want to predict his reaction. First, he wouldn't like losing what I do for him at the statehouse, but having him concerned about possibly being dragged down with me? Uh-uh, no way. You know how volatile he can be."

Senator Sturbridge was beginning to gain back composure. "Frankly, we have tried to keep our association under wraps, but it has gone on so long that it wouldn't be hard to link us together. And he knows it." Heading off the deep end again, the senator's voice broke. "Then there's all the others involved— all respected professional people. Wall Street bankers, lawyers, actors, musicians. I don't want to think where this could lead to. I'm scared, Arkady."

"I see your point, and I share your concern. Senator, you can count on us. We will have this taken care of in short order. We have a plan in the works. You needn't worry yourself further."

"I hope you are right, Arkady. Your friendship means a lot to me. Fix this, and I will owe you big time."

When the call ended, Arkady cradled the phone with disgust. He held it with two fingers, as if it was dirty—as if it would contaminate him. He repeated the senator's words: "I will owe you big time." He smirked and thought, *Those are the words I've been yearning to hear from you, Senator.*

Annika flopped into a side chair and asked, "The good senator again?"

"Yeah, and he's off the rails."

Annika observed, "Maybe if he stuck to the girls and left the little boys alone—"

"Now, sister, this is no time to take offense at the very business we're in. The senator isn't just another wealthy client with a distasteful appetite. He's someone who can move mountains and part seas. He's our 'in' crowd. And we need him ... even if he is a creepy pedophile."

"So what's our next move?" Anika asked.

With his fingers intertwined tightly, Arkady pondered, "I think it may be time to send the twins out again—this time with specific instructions."

"Another screw-up is not an option, brother. I wouldn't want Volkov to get wind of any of this ... considering the last time when the twins went overboard despite your instructions."

"No, it isn't. But it is time to ramp up the heat."

129

"Just a thought … what about using our Lieutenant?"

Arkady reclined in his executive chair and shook his head in wonder. "You know, sister, your strategic thinking amazes me. Of course—he's perfect for this. Besides, it pulls him in deeper."

"Exactly!"

CHAPTER 24

ANGEL STRUGGLED ALL day to think of a way to contact the children without alerting the woman monitor. She came up with a plan, but it would depend on luck to pull it off … lots of luck.

She carefully ascended, firmly gripping each metal rung. *This fire escape ladder scares me. It moves when I do. I wonder how well it's attached to these bricks.* A light breeze came up in mild gusts at first. But it soon grew to a wrathful fury, as if purposefully assigned to dislodge this night's stealthy intruder. The chill wind funneled down the narrow alley and blew her hair askew. With her face scrunched up and eyes squeezed shut, she hugged the ladder so tightly her fingers grew numb. The creaky old ladder resisted nature's force and resolutely clung to the building as it had for nearly a hundred years. She forced herself to continue upward, rung by rung. Her muscles ached, but—drawing upon inner strength—she pushed on. When she reached the top, she reached out blindly and grasped the edge of the catwalk. She shimmied over and collapsed onto the harsh metal. Exhausted and out of breath, she murmured, "Thank you, dear ladder, I will never doubt you again." She was triumphant. She basked in her conquest for a long moment. *I did it. I did it myself!*

She crawled to the storage room's darkened window and pulled the metal bar from her waistband. Just like downstairs, she found she could wedge it into the track of the old window. Using all her strength, she managed to shove the top window sash nearly an inch out of position. She pushed the bar down in between the two sashes and pulled hard. Unlike the sturdy ladder, this old, rusted lock gave up, allowing the window to open. She slowly and carefully crawled over the sill and gingerly put one foot down onto the dark storage room floor.

With both feet on the floor, she waited a terrifying moment, barely breathing. *Did I make too much noise opening the window or sliding over the windowsill?* Except for heartbeats pounding in her ears, the answer came in the form of complete silence followed by her stifled sigh of relief.

In the dimmed light, she fingertip-felt her way along the shelving, desperate to avoid knocking anything over. Concentrating on the shelf contents, her right elbow bumped against a floor lamp, causing it to slowly tilt and head toward the floor. Angel reached out instinctively with her right hand and caught it. Remaining half-bent over, she reverently restored the lamp to its original position.

Like a surgeon carefully threading a catheter through an artery, she slowly made her way to the doorway. On the other side of that door were children being held prisoner. Children that needed her. Children she needed.

This lock is a joke. Just like in anybody's house, she thought. With a smooth but firm movement, she unlocked it and ever so slowly pushed the door forward. The bright lights in the children's room momentarily assaulted her. Through fluttering eyelids, she saw children playing video games and watching television. She saw no sign of the heavy woman monitor, so Angel pushed the door open a little farther ... just two inches or so. She squished her face against the opening and waited.

None of the children were looking in Angel's general direction. None but one, that is. A girl she guessed to be about twelve sat staring at a blank wall, her shoulders drooped, deep in thought. Angel studied her for a moment. Taking a deep breath, she thought, *It's now or never.*

Maintaining a minimal opening, she pushed her hand through and wiggled her fingers. It worked. The young girl caught the movement and frowned, as though she couldn't comprehend someone appearing from behind the storage room door. Angel pushed open the door a little more, exposing her face. She smiled and sent a finger-to-lips shush. Intrigued, the girl came close enough for Angel to reach out and hurriedly usher her inside.

Angel stroked her hair gently and spoke in soothing tones. "Don't be afraid. I am a friend. I am here to help you. Do you speak English?"

Responding to Angel's kindly demeanor, the girl said, "Inglés? Si, un poco … a leetle."

Between Angel's high school Spanish and the girl's limited facility with English, they tediously communicated.

Angel learned her young new friend, Alicia, was eleven years old and an orphan. She was taken while working in a cabbage field near her home in Honduras. Alicia thought it was about two weeks ago, but she wasn't sure. She looked back at the door and said most of the children were from South American countries, but several were Asian. They had spent most of their time in a large truck with only bottled water and fresh fruit to eat. All were frightened, hungry, and tired.

"What has happened to you since you got here?"

"Food is good. La Gorda—the fat nurse—her name is Camila. She shows movies, those porno movies, you know. Los pequeños no entienden, pero yo sí. Oh, sorry … in inglés … the others no understand. I do. Camila say we in school. She say we have better life now."

Angel sat back hard on a bundle of sheets and sighed. "Jeez. I'm so sorry, Alicia. I swear I will help you." They hugged each other tightly.

Angel said, "I am a prisoner too. But I have some ideas. You will see." She explained her own situation, hoping to gain Alicia's complete trust. She warned, "You must not talk about me yet. You must not tell the others. If Camila finds out we talked, we both will be in very bad danger. Mal peligro. ¿Entender? I have to leave now, but I will be back. I don't know when, but I will be back with help."

"I will not tell … te prometo." Alicia paused and whispered, "Por favor, dime su nombre. Umm … your name, please?"

"Angel. My name is Angel."

Alicia's face lit up. She exclaimed, "Si, tu eres mi angel. Umm … you are my angel!" She blessed herself. "You come to save us."

Angel thought, *Kid, if only you knew what kind of angel I am!*

A moment later, from her seat back in the big room, Alicia smiled back at her angel. Both had tears running down their cheeks. Angel sent a shush signal once again. Alicia nodded. With one more look around the room, Angel slowly closed and relocked the storage room door. She thought, *I bet that's the first time that little one's smiled in a long time. Now I gotta get back to my room before somebody misses me.*

Reaching across from the catwalk, she grabbed a rung and said, "Mr. Ladder, don't fail me now. We got more stuff to do."

CHAPTER 25

ARKADY IMPATIENTLY PACED back and forth behind his desk. When Mikels finally arrived an hour late, he said, "What took you so long? When I call you, I want you here now. And don't use the old traffic excuse ... leave earlier."

"Okay. I'll quit the PD and come to work for you full-time. But you won't have access to inside information—information like I have for you today."

Arkady's face gradually brightened into a coy smirk. "What information?"

Mikels explained that a police raid was imminent on a Staten Island drug house. He was unable to provide the exact address, but he was sure it was in the Tottenville section. "Amboy Road was mentioned, so I'm pretty sure that's where it is."

Arkady couldn't conceal his excitement. "Could you find out when? Is it DEA or local?"

"I can't ask questions without jeopardizing everything. But it didn't sound like a DEA operation." Mikels frowned, acting as though he was thinking about how he could contribute more.

Arkady said, "That's okay. That's okay." He excitedly rubbed his hands together and couldn't suppress a chuckle. "This couldn't have come at a better time. Thank you, Gregor!"

In a feigned naive tone, Mikels said, "Sorry I couldn't give more details. Does it mean anything to you?"

"Oh yeah. I know just who will be happy to learn of this. What you've brought me today will put me in good standing with some powerful people. You are proving your worth."

Mikels added, "There's more, although I don't think it applies in any way to you. An undercover sweep of all massage parlors in Manhattan and Queens is on for this weekend. It seems the Koreans are in for a surprise." He shook his head and laughed matter-of-factly.

Arkady took the bait. "Are you kidding me? That's even bigger. You are doing exactly what we want, Gregor." He ripped his cell phone from his pocket and, giggling like a schoolboy, he dialed. "Please tell Mr. Volkov it's Arkady, and I have something important for him." With his hand over the phone, he turned to Mikels and remarked, "This is like pouring cement into a footing.

Favors are the basis—the building blocks. This is how we build relationships."

Mikels's impassive demeanor belied his thoughts. *Yeah, as long as I can keep my tender ass out of those cement footings.*

Arkady spoke into the phone. "Yes, Yuri. Two things: a drug bust is coming on or near Amboy Road soon. And get this … you may tell your Korean friends to keep their act clean this weekend. The heat is coming down on them in Manhattan and Queens." Arkady nodded several times. "Yes, it comes from him." He paused, listening, and rolled his eyes at Mikels. "Of course. But he will only do it through me. I'm sure you understand. This is just a sample of things to come, my friend. Yes, bye-bye." He followed it in Russian to appease Volkov. "Yeah, noka-noka."

Arkady sat tapping his pen and staring at Mikels. "You have done it, Gregor. I couldn't be more pleased. Now, let's see what happens or, should I say, doesn't happen this weekend."

Mikels slid into a side chair. "That's why I'm here, Arkady." The obvious left unspoken, he tilted his head and lifted his eyebrows in anticipation.

Arkady caught the subtlety. He called out loudly, "Annika, bring some cash for our friend. Make it twenty-five hundred."

Mikels smiled broadly. He thought, *This will be our first donation to the Missing and Abused Children's Fund. Worten will like that touch.* Images of a Regal yacht tried to materialize but failed to come into focus.

While handing the envelope to Mikels, Annika commented, "You know, brother, we were talking about giving Gregor another assignment ... our more pressing and unresolved problem. Remember?"

"Yes, yes." Arkady picked up on Annika's lead. He turned to Mikels. "We still need to get that camera memory card. I could send two of my people out again, but they did poorly last time. Even though you ended up with the wrong card, you did perform well. Perhaps you can come up with an idea to handle this without resorting to unpleasant and risky methods."

Mikels felt a rush. *This is it. If I am ever to make contact with Angel, this is my opportunity.* "Well, I have been thinking about that for a while. You know, in my experience, there's nothing like an emotional videotape to compel cooperation when all else fails." Leaving it at that—and hoping Arkady would take it from there—Mikels waited.

It was Annika who spoke up. "Excellent! How 'bout it, my brother. Let's have the lieutenant do his police act and get Angel on tape, pleading with the little jerk for her freedom."

Arkady, ever so slowly, nodded his head and squinted his eyes in agreement. "Yes, that could work. Let's do it."

Mikels and Annika exchanged knowing glances. Both knew it was her idea and that she fed it to her brother.

The little seamstress walked ahead of Mikels toward the end of the hall. She reached into her jacket and retrieved the key to the third-floor stairway. On the climb up, she said, "Missy Ange bery pretty lady but not bery strong, I think. She cry a lot, I think." Suspicious of the new man and forever protective of those in her charge, Rosamie demanded, "Why you see her?"

"Just to talk. I will be making a video too."

Taken aback, Rosamie asked, "You make Missy Ange do porno?"

Mikels stifled a grin and said, "No, no. You could call it, um, a greeting card of sorts."

Standing at Angel's door, Mikels thought back to earlier when he convinced Arkady it would be better to see Angel alone. He argued that, as a person new to her, he would be better positioned to get her cooperation. He said, "She's already had plenty of 'bad cop.' Playing 'good cop' should work after the amount of stress she's been under recently."

Rosamie knocked and yelled, "Missy, man here to see you!"

CHAPTER 26

STARING AT THE floor in front of Angel's door, Mikels and Rosamie waited for a response. Angel slowly opened the door, just enough to tentatively peer out. "What is it? I was asleep. What else can I do around here?"

"This man here to see you, Ange. Annika say you be good."

"Whoa, I ain't no two-bit whore you can crank up on demand. You tell Annika-"

Mikels butted in, "'Whoa' yourself! That's not what this is about. We need to talk about Caleb."

Angel ripped open the door, her eyes blazing. "What about Caleb?"

"Let me in, and we'll talk." They locked eyes for a long moment. Mikels respectfully said, "Please."

Angel slowly backed up, admitting Mikels but with understandable uncertainty.

He turned to Rosamie and said, "Not you."

Rosamie's face darkened. Standing her ground, she demanded, "Why? I responsib for this missy."

"Go ask Annika if you doubt me."

While not satisfied, Rosamie backed away, and Mikels shut the door. "Please, sit on the bed. I will use the chair." Then he shushed Angel and tiptoed back to the door and listened. Hearing Rosamie's breathing on the other side, he slammed his fist sharply against the door and yelled, "Leave. Now!"

A startled Rosamie left, mumbling in her native tongue. Mikels sat down opposite Angel, crossed his legs, and took a deep breath. Before saying anything, he took a moment to study Angel. His first impression was that of a beautiful young woman. Even though she appeared tired and frazzled, her natural good looks came through. Finally, he opened with all he could come up with at the moment. "What a time I've had trying to reach you."

Angel blinked a couple of times. "Who the hell are you, and what do you want?"

"I'm a friend. I'm here to get you out, though at the moment, I'm not sure how to do it."

"Sure, and I'm Mother Teresa."

"Well, so far, you're not what I expected either. According to everyone I've spoken to, you're supposed to be shy, frail, and afraid of everything."

Angel said quietly, "Times are changing. So who are you?"

Mikels took his police ID folder out and handed it to Angel. She opened it and saw a gold badge with blue letters that said, "Linden Police Lieutenant." She turned it sideways, her eyes scanning the identification card with Mikels's photo. Glaring doubtfully at him, she held it up and compared Mikels to the photo. He reached out to retrieve it, but she pulled it back.

He sat back and smiled. "Still not convinced?"

She stuck her fingers into one of the side pouches and pulled out a Linden Police business card with Lieutenant Gregory Mikels's name imprinted on it. Again, she looked up at Mikels suspiciously. She dove deeper into the pouch and came up with another card. It said, "Chief William Worten, Union County Prosecutor's Office."

Angel gulped. "You know Caleb's Uncle Bill?"

"He sent me here … Jelly."

"Oh my God! You are for real."

"Uh-huh. Are you alright?"

"First, tell me about Caleb. He was hurt. His head—it was awful."

"He's fine. We're keeping him safe. These Russians want the camera memory card in exchange for you. We offered them one, but it wasn't the one they wanted, which is how I stumbled into this mess."

Angel angrily shook her head. "I knew it. That stupid scam. I knew it would get us in trouble."

Mikels said, "Look, I don't have a lot of time to chat. I'm here to take a video of you pleading with Caleb to turn over the memory card so you can go home. I have those two downstairs convinced I can get more from you with sugar than vinegar. Get it?"

"Okay. I'll do it but be sure to tell him I'm alright. Really. I'm not who I was. I can handle this."

Mikels picked up on the last part. He squinted and asked, "What? What do you mean by that? We're getting you out of here."

Angel inched closer to the edge of the bed and spoke earnestly. "Listen. There are over twenty little kids one flight up who were brought across the southern border to be sex slaves. I think this is a sort of reception center. From what I learned, they feed them, clean them up, and educate them before selling them off. And I ain't leaving here without them. Understand?"

Mikels's reaction was astonishment. "You are telling me—right here in this building, one floor up—there's a child sex for sale operation going on? Oh my God. I did hear a kid crying!"

"Yup. And I am right in the middle of it."

She went on to tell Mikels of her drugged encounter with Yuri Volkov and her fire escape mission to find the children. She was especially passionate when she described her encounter with Alicia. "I'm not leaving without these kids. No way. You can take that back to Uncle Bill. Tell him to figure something else out. But you better act quick 'cause Rosamie hinted they won't be around here long. I don't like it. I'd guess Volkov and Brighton Beach are involved somehow."

Mikels stood with hands on his hips, staring at the ceiling. "Whew. You've got me bowled over. I came here expecting you to be anxious to get out." "Now I find …"

"I ain't no damsel in distress, Lieutenant. I was. No more." She leaned forward and took Mikels's hand. She said imploringly, "Please, whatever you do, I don't want Caleb to ever know about what I have to do to save these kids. Lieutenant, you don't know me. I've been at the bottom, and if it weren't for Caleb, I wouldn't even be here or anywhere. I'd be dead."

Mikels sat listening, slack-jawed and at a loss for words.

"But I know how to deal with these people. In fact, I'm the perfect one to be here. I can run rings around them. Play with their heads. I've been there—in this, uh, situation—before, but now I have a cause. I'll beat these pricks at their own game." She sat back on the bed. "No. You figure something out. We gotta save these kids. But I'll need my Caleb when this is over, and I don't want to have to go over all the bad stuff again with him. Together, we got past it once. I don't know if he can handle it this time."

Mikels was overwhelmed. "I can't get over you. What do you suggest?" He thought, *You should be asking that of me.*

"I'm not sure. I need to find out more about the transfer. It's soon, I think. Camila, the nurse upstairs, was pecking away on her laptop when I saw her. She was probably making a list of kids and their condition and stuff like that."

"You're suggesting you stay here ... undercover, with no back-up?" Mikels began pacing. "It's out of the question. Do you understand the danger you are in? If you can get to the fire escape, you can get out and let us handle the rest."

Defiantly, she answered, "No can do! And you can't make me, can you?" Her eyes drilled into Mikels's.

Mikels studied Angel, looking for a chink in her armor. *Not there. Jesus, she's strong!*

He surrendered. "Under the circumstances, I suppose not. I could grab you right now, walk you out of here with my gun out, going tough shit on anyone who tries to stop us, and my job would be done. But now you've put me between a rock and a hard place. I'd have those kids on my conscience." He stared at

Angel for a long moment. "Damn you. You read people pretty well, don't you?"

"It's called experience, Lieutenant. Maybe not experience as pure as most people would prefer, but it works just the same. I've lived on the street. I know how to survive. You're a cop, do I have to draw you a picture?"

"Okay, okay, I follow. I hope you know what you're doing." Mikels took out his iPhone and readied it. "Now, let's get this video out of the way."

Angel was convincing. She requested to be seated on the chair instead of the bed, relieving any insinuation Caleb might take from it. When they reviewed the tape, Mikels was satisfied.

"You did great … shoulda been an actress."

"That wasn't acting. I do want out of here, but—"

"Yeah, I know. Don't rub it in. I'm gonna have a hard enough time selling your staying here to Worten and the rest of them. Especially Caleb."

"Your job, not mine." Angel paused and asked, "Would you mind making another quick video? This one is for Caleb … so he'll understand. He needs to hear it from me and to know I'll be okay."

Mikels added a second video segment, then immediately sent it to his home computer and deleted it from his iPhone in case Arkady inspected his phone. He commented, "There's no way we can communicate either. No cell phone. No internet access. Any ideas, Jelly?"

"My only connection to the outside world is that fire escape. But I can't take the chance of being away from here for too long, ya know?"

Mikels came up with an idea. "Let's just suppose I could get a cell phone up onto that fire escape for you to use, with auto-dialing programmed to make it easy to reach me."

"Sounds good, but how would you attach it? How would I find it? And let me tell you, that ladder is rickety. Whoever brings it up better be a lightweight and gutsy acrobat to get up the fire escape from below. It's a lot easier for me once I get past the window."

His mind in organizational mode, Mikels said, "We can put it in a small black magnetized box and attach it somewhere safe near the hall window you use. Maybe there's a spot underneath and out of sight that you could feel around for it. That way, no one else could find it."

Angel said, "Okay, that would work. Make sure it's charged."

"Good point. How about we put a small portable charger in with it? You could keep it plugged in when you're not using it."

Angel slowly nodded in agreement. "Sounds like a plan coming together."

Mikels got up to leave. He extended his hand, but to his surprise, Angel brushed his hand aside and hugged him. She whispered, "You're the angel, Lieutenant. Please ... remember the kids!"

His arms awkwardly posed, reaching beyond Angel, he laughed and said, "I'm no angel either. You'll find that out one of these days."

CHAPTER 27

Eric Sullivan's cabin in Pennsylvania.

CALEB SHOT UPRIGHT from his cot. "What the hell was that?"

"Oh, that's just Big Louie. He sounds off just before six every morning." Eric cracked another egg into the pan.

Caleb squinted through sleepy eyelids out the back window of the cabin. There he was: Big Louie, strutting among his harem of hens, periodically crowing to let all within earshot know who was boss like the male chauvinist rooster that he was.

"Jesus, it's the middle of the night. Do you get up this early every day?"

"Yes, and while you're here, it's *we* who get up this early every day. You'll get used to it."

Caleb stepped out onto the front porch and stretched. The first rays of sunlight were tentatively peeking through the tree limbs, dismissing darkness and making for another slice of life

151

in the woods. A slight shiver caught Caleb by surprise. *I'm never up this early,* he thought. *Why would I be?*

"Bacon and eggs are on, Caleb. Better get in here before the dogs beat you to it."

After working all morning with Eric, cutting firewood with a two-man bucksaw and digging a drainage ditch leading away from the hen house, they took a break.

Caleb asked, "Eric, why would you want to live way out here in the woods?" He dramatically held his arms out and slowly spun around. "No people. No nothing."

Eric poked a small stick around in his pipe, loosening ash and making it ready for a smoke. He said, "I don't see it the same way you do, Sonny. I see it as freedom from the complications of city life. It's freedom from people and their petty nonsense. Most of all, it allows me to make my own choices without having to live up to what others expect of me."

"I hear you on the last one, for sure. I have to ask—and I hope you don't mind—do you ever feel bitter about … you know, your injury and the guys that did it?"

"I did at first. Then I realized all I was doing was carrying them around with me. They were dead, but they were winning the fight inside me, turning me bitter. But I caught on. Instead of feeling sorry for myself, I shoved them overboard, and—" he smiled and said, "I decided to build a hen house."

"But what about the guys that did it to you? I'd never go a day without thinking about them and what they did to me."

"I suppose I could've felt that way, but then they'd still own me, wouldn't they? They already own my kneecap. Nothing more. No siree, Bob! Besides, they're dead and gone. They paid up."

Caleb studied his host carefully. "It almost sounds like you've forgiven them."

"I guess. In a way, that's true. What's to be gained by holding on to bad stuff that happens to you? Life is what it is. There's good and bad. I've learned to hold the good close and screw the bad. If it takes forgiveness to do that, well then, I can do that." He lit his pipe and paused before delivering a hard point. "It's not as if you're sacrificing something when you forgive. It doesn't cost you anything, right? What you're doing is driving out thoughts, memories, and demons that haunt you. Why should I let them possess me?"

"But how can you forgive and forget somebody screwing up your leg?"

"Forget? No, I can't forget. I live with this stiff leg every day. It's just there. But the forgiving part works, believe me. I told myself, 'You can't let other folks and their own messed-up lives define who you are.' I got a life of my own, so I get on with it."

Caleb's reaction was a thousand-yard stare. Slowly shaking his head, he declared, "Some things are unforgivable."

Seeing something in the kid worth pursuing, Eric wasn't about to let it go. "They may be unforgivable today—maybe not tomorrow. Caleb, time has its purpose. On one hand, time takes its toll on everybody; on the other hand, it tends to bring focus." He chuckled. "The trick is to get your ass into focus before you run out of time."

Back at their chores, Caleb was deep in thought. He saw through Eric's preaching and knew the topic of that conversation wasn't finished. Still ... he could never forgive his father. *That ain't gonna happen!*

CHAPTER 28

Linden Police Headquarters.

"CHIEF, YOU GOTTA be kidding. I'm in the middle of a serious undercover operation, and you want me to go back to school? I can't believe this!" Mikels was aghast.

Linden Chief Collins was unrelenting. "Greg, this *is* about your undercover investigation. Chief Worten called and wants you there. You can pull yourself away for just one day, can't you?"

With a sigh, Mikels said, "Let's see: two chiefs against one lieutenant. The outcome seems clear."

"Right. Go!"

Kean College, Union, NJ - Criminal Justice Program.

Chief Worten and Greg Mikels shared a brief glance of recognition across the classroom. They'd agreed to stay apart and not jeopardize the investigation by drawing attention to their relationship.

Worten cautioned, "No sense taking a chance; if one cop could be compromised, others could too."

Attendees who filed into the room were from other Union County police agencies, the New Jersey State Police, several Kean University criminal justice graduate students, and a small group of social workers.

Following the program director's welcoming remarks, Dr. Jonathan Orin opened his talk entitled, "Sex and Souls for Sale."

"Good morning. We are here to discuss a difficult subject. You and the general public might not be comfortable accepting the idea, but many children around the world—and yes, right here in New Jersey—are victims of child sex traffickers. It is here, ladies and gentlemen, and it needs to be exposed. My purpose today is to acquaint you with an overall view of child sex trafficking, including its victims, its perpetrators and their methods, and how law enforcement should respond."

Dr. Orin continued speaking as he clicked off corresponding slides from his PowerPoint program. "First, what is child sex trafficking? It is when a child under the age of eighteen is forced in a variety of ways into a situation of dependency on their trafficker and is used by that trafficker to provide sexual services to customers for a profit. Child sex trafficking activity is broken down into three types of sex trafficking crimes: acquisition, transportation, and exploitation. Sex trafficking, whether child or adult, is one of the biggest criminal businesses in the world.

The United Nations 2019 Trafficking in Persons Report declared that 24.9 million people around the world are victims of human trafficking. In terms of transnational trafficking, North America is a prime destination for significant flows from countries in Central America and the Caribbean."

Dr. Orin went on to discuss human trafficking in other countries, the most significant in terms of numbers being India and China. "In those countries, it is not uncommon for children to be sold into sex slavery by their parents."

A Kean student raised his hand and asked, "But how do they get away with it here in this country? I have a hard time believing there's widespread child sex trafficking in America."

Dr. Orin answered, "While a small percentage is local and may be operated by a pimp, most activity takes place within the confines of organized crime. In other words, criminal syndicates—one kind of 'mafia' or another. For example, the Russian mob is at work in casinos and brothels in Europe and Asia, as well as in twenty-seven states in the U.S., conducting human trafficking. Prostitution has become the preferred crime for the Russian mafia due to the high-profit margin."

The Kean student, assiduously taking notes, followed up with, "Where in the U.S. is it most prevalent?"

"Here, it takes place mostly in the Miami, Florida and New York City areas … more particularly, in Brighton Beach."

Mikels couldn't resist turning his head to glance at Chief Worten, whose eyes met his. Worten nodded slowly, almost imperceptibly. Mikels thought, *I guess I know now why I'm here today.*

The program continued with Dr. Orin detailing important statistics relating to human trafficking in the U.S. He relied upon information supplied by UNITAS—an international organization devoted to combating trafficking since 2015—and put bullets on the screen:

… Numbers: An estimated 400,000 people are currently living in modern-day slavery in the U.S.—which includes labor trafficking and sex trafficking, as well as debt bondage and forced marriage.

… Gender: According to a 2016 DOJ-funded study of youth (aged thirteen through twenty-four) involved in the sex trade (which includes sexual exploitation and survival sex, as well as human trafficking) across six different cities in the U.S., 60 percent were female, 36 percent were male, and 4 percent were transgender.

... Age: In 2017, the nationwide, FBI-led anti-trafficking raid-Operation Cross Country (OCC)-reported the average age of sex trafficking victims in October of that year was fifteen years old, but the youngest were two years and three months old.

... Labor/sex: Of the forms of human trafficking reported to the National Human Trafficking Hotline in 2017, 71 percent were for sex trafficking, 15 percent for labor trafficking, 4 percent for cases of both sex and labor trafficking, and 10 percent where the trafficking was unspecified.

Dr. Orin summed up the morning program with the words of Lubo Krstajic of UNITAS: "Human trafficking happens in every state in the U.S. and is happening right now. Victims can get recruited into human trafficking through force, fraud, or coercion. It often involves the promise of a better life in one way or another. Human trafficking is under-reported for many reasons, so precise numbers are difficult to come by. Here at UNITAS, we are forging partnerships with governments, non-government organizations, and experts in the field to develop collaborative solutions in the fight against human trafficking of all kinds."

Before dismissing the class for lunch, Dr. Orin said, "This afternoon, we will discuss how traffickers work and how law enforcement should respond. But I want to leave you this morning with an observation by Irish statesman and philosopher Edmund Burke: 'The only thing necessary for the triumph of evil is for good men to do nothing.' Think about it."

During the lunch break, Worten and Mikels managed to have a few words in the food line. Mikels commented to Worten, "This class should be standard in the academy. I wish my people knew all this."

Worten reached for a roll and agreed. "I'm going to be looking into it."

During the afternoon program, another speaker explained how sex trafficking happens behind the scenes in just about all of society.

"People have always sought out sex in venues such as massage parlors, escort services, and streetwalkers, but it is the internet where most solicitation for sex occurs nowadays. It has grown exponentially since the internet. From high schoolers to celebrities, people are sexting and breaking down sexual taboos, leaving many vulnerable to blackmail and pressure to perform sexual acts to be accepted. Most children are exposed to porn by ages eight to twelve, and most young adults watch it regularly. Porn is used by traffickers to teach children how to have sex and to 'normalize' sexual abuse."

When the afternoon class began to cover law enforcement methods to address trafficking, Worten and Mikels discreetly left. There would be nothing new there for them. But they sat in Worten's car for a few minutes and talked.

Mikels said, "Chief, I'm glad you brought me here for this. It brings everything into focus for me and gives me added motivation to put Spasibo and Volkov behind bars where they belong."

"Don't forget the customers, Greg—those who pay for sex with kids. We're gonna be turning up the heat on them too. I don't care who they are. Some big shots are taking a fall soon, you'll see. But to really have an impact, we must hit them from all sides: both supply and demand."

CHAPTER 29

Brighton Beach, Brooklyn, New York.

YURI VOLKOV'S THREE-ACRE mansion and property backed up to the Brighton Beach seawall. The house was airy, spacious, and, above all, ostentatious. Upon entering the long driveway from Brightwater Court, Mikels and Arkady were greeted by a green and gold leaf designer sign: "American Dacha by the Sea." Volkov's skeet shooting exhibition was underway, indicated by a deep thumping reverberation of shotgun rounds coming from behind the house.

Yuri Volkov stood at the ready, his .12-gauge shotgun pointed down-range and out over the waters of Lower New York Bay. He readied himself and yelled, "Pull!" Two clay birds, one from either direction, crossed in front of him, only to be demolished in quick succession.

As Volkov lowered the weapon, he turned to approaching Arkady and said, "Poof. Just like in old Soviet Union, no?"

Arkady offered a weak smile. "Yeah, poof." *Your favorite word.* Not yet introduced to Volkov, Mikels stood awkwardly off to one side, closely examining the collection of guns displayed on a nearby table.

Volkov ejected the shell casings and walked Arkady over toward Mikels with one hand on the younger Russian's shoulder. He remarked, "You know, Arkady, you have a great future with me. You just have to understand what sharing is." He extended a hand, saying, "You must be our lieutenant."

Mikels returned a sniper-rifle he was inspecting to the table and looked up. "Nice shooting. Nice collection too." They shook hands.

Volkov hefted the Fabbri over-and-under .12-gauge and said, "Oh yeah, especially this one. You could buy a Lamborghini for what I paid for it, but it's worth it." Offering the shotgun to Mikels, he said, "Wanna give it a try?"

Mikels said, "Thanks, but I prefer my Glock 22." He pulled back his jacket, revealing his shoulder-holstered service automatic. "A .40 caliber S&W round has great stopping power and fifteen rounds. But it's intended for different kinds of birds."

Volkov said jokingly, "Like jailbirds, Lieutenant?" They all laughed.

Mikels figured this firearm session was Volkov's way of leading up to something … something that required a macho setting. He figured right.

"Gregor—you don't mind me calling you Gregor, do you?" Volkov took Mikels's arm and began walking him away from Arkady, who had relegated himself to pacing back and forth along the sea wall, feigning interest in beached mollusks.

"Of course not. That was my grandfather's name for me."

"Well then, Gregor it is. You know, your recent performance was right on. In Tottenville, the narcs came up empty, and my Korean friends owe me a big favor."

"My pleasure." Mikels glanced back at Arkady, who was standing rather forlornly, still pretending interest in critters along the shoreline.

Volkov continued, still with his hand on Mikels's shoulder, "Gregor, I would like you to work for me. I understand from Arkady—" he motioned Arkady over— "that you prefer to only work through him. And I get the simplicity of doing it that way. But, you see, I like direct contact." He squeezed Mikels's shoulder to the muscle. "I like to look into someone's eyes when I talk to them. Understand?"

Mikels saw a look of panic on Arkady's face. He brought the stroll to a halt and responded, "I, uh … I think we should come to an understanding here. I appreciate your comments—and hey, who doesn't want to be wanted, right?" He laughed nervously. "But my concern is having too many masters. I already have two: the department and Arkady. Diluting the pecking order further complicates things."

"'Too many masters.' Hmm … a good way of putting it." Volkov clasped his hands behind his back and gestured for Mikels and Arkady to follow him. "When I was promoted from a major in the Soviet Army to a colonel in the KGB, I ran into a guy you may have heard of. Vladimir Putin. You could say we were colleagues of sorts. Although, he had more of a keen understanding of Communist Party politics than I did."

Shaking his head almost imperceptibly, Arkady shot a cautioning look at Mikels that said, *Don't interrupt.*

Volkov went on. "This was a time when Gorbachev was caving in to Reagan and the Central Committee had grown from seventy-one members to nearly three hundred. Gorbachev saw the end of the Soviet Union on the horizon due to America outspending us militarily. We just couldn't keep up with America's powerhouse economy. Gorbachev wasn't a weak man, but he was more pragmatic than many in the politburo thought necessary."

Volkov sighed stoically as he reminisced. "1991 was a very bad year and a very good year. Boris Yeltsin and his crew made my decision for me. My gut said, 'Get out.' I did."

Volkov stopped walking. He looked into Mikels's eyes and said, "You speak of too many masters? You have no idea, Gregor, what it is to have too many masters. I had three hundred masters. It was a nightmare." Abruptly, his mood changed. He stopped and lifted both arms to the sky. In his deep voice, he bellowed, "Which is why I am here in sunny Brighton Beach, pursuing the American dream!" He leaned forward and said in a near-whisper, "Or, as they say, 'Follow the money!'" He laughed hoarsely at his attempt at humor, nearly choking on phlegm.

Mikels thought, *Yeah, you and Al Capone.*

Arkady caught Mikels's eye again. His head was tilted slightly, his lips mockingly pursed, and eyes wide. All of which conveyed, *I've heard this bullshit before ... just hang in there.*

His laughter having drained away, Volkov continued blustering. "Putin's star began to rise. When someone got in his way? He didn't hesitate. They were gone. Poof! I studied him. He could smile at you in such a sincere way, then stab you in the throat before you knew it. You were ... poof! He got where he was going. He's still there. Know what I mean?" It wasn't a rhetorical question. He expected an answer.

Mikels reacted carefully. "Uh-huh. He's on top."

"I learned much from Putin ... about loyalty." Volkov stood very still and slowly nodded his head, his penetrating eyes glued to Mikels's. He was demanding a better answer.

Grasping the nature of the test, Mikels half-smiled. "I get it, Yuri—may I call you Yuri?"

Volkov assented with a single, impatient nod.

"Yeah, I get it." The threat vividly clear, Mikels looked resolutely into Volkov's eyes and said, "No loyalty? Poof!"

Volkov turned to Arkady and grinned widely. "He gets it. Okay, we'll do it your way." As they slowly walked, Volkov rubbed his hand between Mikels's shoulder blades. "But I want to be kept aware of everything that goes on. No screw-ups. We have too much to lose." He glanced over his shoulder at Arkady following along behind. "When I need something done, like a favor—you know what I mean by 'a favor,' Arkady?—I expect prompt service."

"No problem, Yuri. And thank you for your understanding." Arkady was relieved despite his not-so-subtle chastisement.

Volkov acknowledged Arkady's kowtowing with, "Hmm." He paused, then asked, "By the way, Arkady, is your shipment ready for transfer?"

"Yes, soon."

Volkov asked, "Are they in good shape?"

Arkady was emphatic. "Absolutely. Camila is doing her job."

Volkov said, "Good." Affecting a sour face, he went on, "Since I'm sharing Gregor, you might do me the courtesy of transferring Angel when the others come over. I enjoyed our last visit. It's a fair trade." Palms up, as if alternately weighing an air-appraisal, he teased, "Let's see. Angel for Gregor." He chuckled. "Yes, I like that. A fair trade."

Volkov turned away, missing the panic-stricken reactions from Mikels and Arkady.

Driving from Volkov's parking lot, Arkady said, "Whew! See what I must put up with? The man is shrewd and dangerous. He's also my protector. Without him, Annika and I would be on our own and very vulnerable. The Koreans and Chinese would move in so fast—"

Mikels interjected, "Yeah. I see what you mean. He's quite full of himself, isn't he? He enjoys talking in circles—circles that look more like targets."

Arkady laughed. "No pun intended, of course."

"And what's with the touchy-feely bit? Is that part of his intimidation routine?"

Arkady explained, "That's old-school Russian. My poppa did it too. It's their way of showing warmth … being personable. Our generation doesn't need it. We're all too sensitive as it is."

After a short pause, Mikels took a chance. Considering Arkady's mood, and feeling a sense of comradery rising, he probed, "So what's being transferred along with Angel? I think I know, but—" he twisted to face Arkady and said sincerely, "I believe I've proven myself to you, Arkady. It's time you were straight with me."

Keeping his eyes on the traffic, Arkady leaned toward Mikels and said in a mock conspiratorial tone, "We have a very lucrative thing going. Ever hear of sex trafficking? We do all kinds, but the best is kids from underdeveloped countries. Annika and I set up a kind of reception center. We handle incomings in the New York area. We clean them up, feed them, do a medical check, and put clothes on their backs. It sounds bad to some people, Gregor, but let me tell you, when we're done with them, these kids never had it so good. All they have to do is make very rich weirdos happy." Arkady laughed. "It's a piece of cake … no pun intended."

Revolted, Mikels felt his pulse quicken. For a flashing moment, he was back in Dr. Orin's sex trafficking class. He wanted to strangle Arkady then and there. Instead, he forged on. "And Volkov's role in all this is …?"

"The boss. Even the Asians respect Volkov. He has the right connections. Remember Epstein? Well, Yuri has the same kind of contacts in that twisted world of well-healed, upper society pervs with too much time on their hands. There are actors, politicians, bankers … you name it. Personally, I don't go there. It's not my thing, but if there's a market for it, why not go for it? That's my philosophy. And Volkov is also positioned well for international deals. Let's suppose you're an Arab sheik—a lonely Arab sheik, if you catch my drift—deal done!"

"So, he puts the deals together? He knows the buyers?"

"Whadda you think? And, being the godfather of all human trafficking in New York, he gets a cut of every sale, leaving those under him to deal with expenses. What a sweet racket."

Arkady changed the subject and spoke soberly, "You do realize our more immediate problem is turning Angel over to him, right? She cannot tell him about Caleb and the missing memory card. The man is unforgiving. It's bad enough that we messed up, but if Volkov finds out—let me put it this way: the last group that crossed him is gone."

"Gone … like in 'poof'?"

"Yeah, all four of them."

Arkady went on to explain Senator Sturbridge's situation and why they had good reason for Volkov not to hear about that slip-up. "You seem to have developed a good relationship with Angel. You know … your 'good cop' thing. Maybe you could convince her to keep quiet?"

"Sure. I'll reason with her. Suppose I put it to her this way: 'If you ever want to see Caleb again …' and so forth. But what if Volkov questions how Angel came to be with you? What then?"

"Come up with something," Arkady smirked. "That's why I pay you the big bucks."

Mikels's head was swimming. *So many moving parts ... how do I tell Angel what's ahead? Is she up to it? She'll be happy to be near the kids, but will we be able to communicate? What will Worten say? And finally, the big question: What the hell is our end game?*

Arkady interrupted Mikels's reverie. "Now that you have met Volkov, what do you think?"

Slumped low in the passenger seat, Mikels gazed through his window at the small Brighton Beach shops passing by with all their signs in Russian. *Christ, this could be any street in Moscow!* Calmly, and without hesitation, he answered, "I think if we fuck up—poof!"

Arkady urged the big Mercedes onto Shore Parkway and snickered. "Yeah, Yuri and his ridiculous 'poof'!"

CHAPTER 30

―――――――――――

IT RAINED. ANGEL didn't dare go to the fire escape and leave wet footprints on the way back to her room. She agonized over the children, knowing they could be moved at any time. She also yearned for the security that planted cell phone would afford … if only in her mind. That is, if it was there.

The next night, she waited until all was quiet and tiptoed to the hall window. Grateful that the broken lock had not been discovered, she pulled herself out onto the fire escape and took several deep breaths. It took only a minute to locate the box affixed to the metal floor beneath her. Safely back in her room, she powered up the cheap burner phone. There was a text message waiting.

It was from Mikels. *Jelly, bad/good news. U R moving to B Bch w/Volk. Kids too. Very soon! Take phone with if u can. Will keep touch. GM*

Angel sat back, took a deep breath, and blew out forcefully. *Okay, game on. I can play that old Ruskie fool for all he's worth. I know what he wants. Been there, done that. It's the kids I'm worried about.* She thought of Alicia, and a lump formed in her throat. *Don't fall apart now, Jelly,* she told herself. *Come up with a plan.*

She answered Mikels's text with *Got it. Good news! Will keep in touch. Pray!*

"Pray? Hmph!" Worten was not impressed. "We're gonna need more than prayer to get through this. What's the plan, Greg? Do we have one?" The veteran chief of county detectives was not one to go forward blindly.

Mikels went over all the details of his afternoon with Arkady and Volkov. Worten listened attentively and made notes. He asked, "What do you think? I think we have enough to move on them, but should we? That's the sixty-four-thousand-dollar question."

"Chief, the way I see it, we want to get Volkov and take down his whole organization. Busting Arkady and Annika? Small timers. Volkov is the big shot of New York sex trafficking. He should be our target."

"Agreed. Go on."

"Let's let it play out a little longer. I'm in tighter than ever with Arkady, and Angel will be on the inside with Volkov soon. We won't get another setup like this in a hundred years."

Worten chewed on his lower lip. He leaned against his windowsill and searched the sky for an answer to their dilemma. "Oh, man! We're damned if we do and damned if we don't. You do know, Greg, we'll be held responsible if anything happens to that girl. But on the other hand, what about all those little kids being brutalized?" He shook his head in disgust.

Mikels offered, "As I see it, we can pull Angel out any time by just muscling in and taking her. But we'd be sacrificing our case against that mob. Maybe we could rescue those kids that way too, but then we wouldn't have a solid case against Volkov, right?

And how many more hundreds or thousands of kids would become victims if he went free? No ... we need to take down the whole bunch. And that includes as many creeps we can identify who buy or rent those kids for sex too."

Worten slumped down into his chair. "Oh, I suppose one could argue that Angel would be our witness as to the presence of the children on the fourth floor ... yadda, yadda. But so what?

And if she is all we have, any good defense attorney could easily impugn her testimony, especially with her sketchy background. You could corroborate her statements and add some of your own observations, but I'd like to see a stronger case, and I know any prosecutor would too."

Mikels reasoned, "That's right. We need more. From what she's hinted, Angel's background is just what she needs to pull this off, Chief. She's one tough cookie, let me tell ya."

He decided to play the second video segment for Worten. It opened with Angel sitting in the same chair, but with an entirely different demeanor. She smiled at the camera, and—unlike in the first video—she no longer had that pathetic look. No longer was she pleading for her release. No longer acting the victim, Angel's voice was strong and unwavering.

"This is for my Caleb and everybody trying to get me out of here. Thank you, but I want you to know I'm okay. I haven't been physically abused. You need to understand that I cannot leave here without a group of children these people are about to sell for sex. I've seen them. I met secretly with one who told me how they got here and that they are in training. Sex training for kids—can you believe it? So I will do what I can here. Please, please, save these kids. Love ya, Cal!"

Worten and Mikels remained silent for a long moment. Chief Worten cleared his throat, laboriously pulled himself upright, and reluctantly agreed. "Okay, then. That's it. I'll prepare a summary of all this, and we'll see what happens next. I'm not comfortable with her in there, but it's the hand we're dealt. I'll say this—she doesn't act like the sob-sister portrayed by Caleb. Let's hope she's tough enough." He squirmed uncomfortably in his chair. "One more thing: I'm sorry, Greg, but I have to bring in the FBI and maybe the local district attorney in New York before we get in over our heads legally. But I'll insist control stays right here with me."

Mikels's pained look wasn't lost on Worten.

"I know, I know. I'll keep those in on it tight for now."

To ease his momentary frustration, Mikels quipped, "Just think, Chief, were it not for those two P.I.s and their clever move on me—instead of playing superhero—right now, I'd be sporting Gucci shades and basking in the Florida sun on my yacht. I was gonna name it 'Spasibo.'"

They shared a blank stare for a few seconds before they both burst out laughing. Chief Worten picked up a notepad on his desk and threw it at Mikels. "Get outta here, wise guy!"

CHAPTER 31

ERIC SULLIVAN CALLED out to Caleb, "Hey, I'm going to town for supplies. Wanna come?"

"Are you kiddin'? Just try and leave me behind!"

The two bounced down the dirt drive in Sullivan's old pick-up truck, and twenty minutes later, they pulled up in front of the 507 Country Store near Paupack. Caleb wandered through the aisles, soaking up anything not related to trees, firewood, and roosters crowing. He had a thought. "Hey, Eric, I'll be out in the truck."

Eric, in neighborly conversation with the owner, waved in agreement and turned away. Nearing Eric's truck, Caleb powered up his cell phone and got a signal. Pleased with his decision to try, he dialed. *Gotta find out what's goin' on back there.*

Nezzie answered. "Mackey Investigations, how can we help you?"

"Nezzie, it's Caleb. Is Mack there?"

"Oh, hi, Caleb. No, Mack's in court today. Is there anything I can do?"

"Well, I just wanted to know what's goin' on. Have they figured out where Jelly is?"

Nezzie wasn't sure what to say. She stalled. "I know that Lieutenant Mikels is making progress, but I don't get to hear it all."

Caleb pushed harder. "But have they found her? I'm out here in left field, and no one is telling me anything. Please."

Nezzie, still feeling that soft spot for Caleb, said, "I think they know where she is. But from what I understand, she won't come out because of … something like children in danger. It's somewhere in Brooklyn, I think. Don't quote me on any of this. I just pick up bits and pieces."

Caleb hung up and called Chief Worten.

"Uncle, I just learned you found Jelly … uh, Angel. Why can't you pull her out? And don't jazz me, please."

"Caleb. Where are you?"

"Still up here in Hicksville. Give it to me straight, Uncle."

Worten sighed. "Okay. She is still being held. They have her in Brooklyn in an abandoned school, but we know she's okay. Mikels has met with her and tried to get her to come out, but she refused."

"What? What the hell are you talking about?"

"I know. It sounds crazy. Ya see, there are kids being held there too, and she won't come out without them. She's one tough cookie."

Caleb was incredulous. "Are you kiddin' me? Angel is borderline helpless. She can't make decisions. She's totally dependent on me, for Chrissake."

"Nope. You're wrong, my boy. She's not the girl you knew. She's tough as nails. I need to show you a video she made, and maybe you'll understand. I did my best, but she won't come out without the kids too."

Caleb shouted, "So why don't you go get her and the kids? Duh!"

"We can't just yet. We're working on it. In the meantime, Mikels has a phone connection with her, but we don't know how long that will last. The whole thing is fluid."

Caleb let it all out. "I can't believe you would let this happen! First, my old man bugs out on me, and now, you do the same. Eric and his forgiveness crap? My ass! You're all the same."

"Whoa, hold it, junior. That's not what this is about. It's a criminal investigation—a big one, at that—and your girlfriend has put us all in a tough position. Just cool down and think a minute."

179

Caleb hung up and slid over into the driver's seat just as Eric came out of the store. Caleb cranked up the old truck and hollered through an open window, "Sorry, Eric. Gotta go. My Jelly is in trouble, and these cop assholes aren't doing a thing about it!" With tires spinning in the dirt, Caleb bounced out onto the road, leaving Eric leaning on his cane, shaking his head.

Eric immediately called Higgins. "Bob? Eric here. The kid bugged out with my truck. I saw he was on his cell phone just before he took off. Sorry—I couldn't stop him."

Bob said, "You know, I thought about it later … I shoulda grabbed his cell phone when I left. Okay, how long ago was it?"

"Less than ten minutes."

"Can you get ahold of the local troopers up there and file a stolen truck report? Maybe we have time to—"

"Right away. I wanted to alert you first."

Bob thought out loud a moment. "I wonder who he called. Chief Worten? Mack? I'll check on that. Keep me posted if the troopers catch up with him."

"Will do. Really sorry, Bob. I didn't think he'd bolt. Something on that phone call put him over the edge."

"Yeah, it's not your fault, pal. I told you he was a problem. I'll get back with you. Bye." Frustrated, Bob slammed the steering wheel. *Now we have Caleb on the loose and Angel being moved with those kids to who knows where and what. We gotta get this mess under control before someone gets hurt!* He started making calls.

CHAPTER 32

"BRIGHTON BEACH? WHY am I going there?" Angel played her part to the hilt.

Annika explained, "It's simple. Yuri Volkov gets what Yuri Volkov wants-and he wants you."

Mikels stood quietly to the side, awaiting his cue.

Angel frowned. "Just what does that mean?"

"Come now, Angel. Don't you remember your last visit with him? It wasn't that bad, was it?" Annika grinned slyly.

"Oh, that." Angel slumped back on her bunk. "If I … you know … does it mean I will be let go soon?"

Annika deferred to Mikels. He stepped forward and said, "Angel, that's up to you. If you follow our instructions—and I mean to a T—you will get home sooner. If you don't … well, you may never get home." He paused and said, "And then there's Caleb's welfare to consider."

"Huh?" Angel appeared confused. "You have Caleb too?"

"No, no. Pay attention." Drawing closer, Mikels leaned in on Angel. "As long as you do as you are told, Caleb will be safe, and you'll get out of here sooner." Unseen by Annika, he winked at Angel.

Angel replied, "I'll do anything to protect Caleb." She began to tear up. "I just don't know why all this is happening to me."

Mikels kept at it. He laughed sarcastically. "Oh yes, you do. You remember that little extortion scam you and Caleb had going, don't you? By now, you've figured it out. You screwed with the wrong people, and it's payback time."

"I'm sorry!" Angel cried. "We never meant to get involved this deep. It was just to make a few bucks, and—"

"Yeah, well, you are in deep now." Mikels pointed a threatening finger at her. "You will not mention Caleb or your scam to Mr. Volkov. Is that clear?"

Angel blinked, puzzled. "What does he care?"

"Never mind about that. Are you gonna do as you're told?"

Angel bowed her head and whispered, "Yeah, I guess."

"Just to be clear, Angel, if you shoot your mouth off, both you and Caleb will disappear." Mikels raised his voice. "Got it?"

Over tear-stained cheeks, she looked up at Mikels and said, "Okay. Okay, I understand."

"For your sake, I hope so. If Mr. Volkov should ask how you came to be with us, you will tell him you were working a modeling job and got high one night, and you don't remember anything more."

"I understand. Please, don't hurt Caleb," she pleaded.

"It's all on you, Angel."

Annika and Mikels turned to leave, but it was Angel's turn to make a demand. She spoke quickly and with apprehension. "I'll do what you say, but only if I get to work with the children when I'm there."

Annika stopped abruptly. "What did you say?"

"You heard me. I'll cooperate. But only if— "

"I heard you. How did you know the children were going to the beach too?"

Angel shrugged and matter-of-factly said, "Rosamie. We talk a lot."

Annika's anger was rising, but before she lost it, Mikels stepped in and scolded Angel.

"You're in no position to make demands," he touched Annika's arm to quiet her and continued, "but if you hold your end up, we'll ask Mr. Volkov for that favor."

Mikels steered Annika out of the room and explained, "This is good. She is motivated by a threat and by favors. It couldn't be better. She'll do all right. Trust me."

As Annika and Mikels descended to the first floor, she said, "Well done, Lieutenant. Your police experience dealing with people comes in handy." She stopped on the steps and scolded Mikels. "But remember who's in charge here. Be careful you don't overstep in your decision-making ideas." She paused, then added, "You're in control all the time, aren't you?"

Mikels shrugged it off. "It comes naturally when you deal with drug addicts every day."

Annika marveled, "Motivation is a wonderful thing, isn't it?"

"Yeah, I suppose." He smirked and thought, *You have no idea, Annika. Not a clue!*

Mikels left Brooklyn and drove to Volkov's house in Brighton Beach. He found Volkov lounging in a recliner on the patio over-looking Lower New York Bay. He was smoking a Cuban cigar and enjoying a Remy Martin XO. He waved Mikels past the security goon stationed near the gate.

Volkov grinned and held up the drink, saying, "There's nothing like a good cognac before dinner. Have one?"

Mikels presented a friendly, albeit patient, smile. "No thanks, Yuri."

"Does Arkady know you're here?"

"No."

Grinning shrewdly, Volkov said, "I've been waiting for this. I knew you were smart … the way you manipulated me into that 'fair trade' scenario." He pulled the recliner upright, blew on the end of the cigar, and with a confident air, said, "So let's have it."

Feigning self-consciousness, Mikels said, "Well now, you're very perceptive, Yuri. You've stolen my thunder, as the saying goes. Yes, I am here to take the next natural step in our … uh, bargain … for lack of a better word."

"Go on, Gregor. I think I am going to enjoy this."

"In short, I think we would be better off if I switched allegiances. That is, I should work principally for you and secondarily for Spasibo. Arkady and Annika are okay, but they're young. They have a long way to catch up to you and your experience. I could be much more helpful to you right here, rather than at a long distance, don't you think?"

Straining to sit upright as he straddled the recliner, Volkov said, "Could it be that you see more money here too?"

Mikels shrugged, continuing his near-apologetic act. "Of course, there's that. But don't you see the simplicity of direct contact versus an intermediary situation? Besides, do you want someone screening information before it gets to you?"

"Of course, I agree." Volkov flicked another flurry of ash. "Consider it done. I will call Arkady and inform him of our decision. He won't like it. Back in the Motherland, we say 'Takova zhizn,' meaning 'that's life.' He'll get over it. But Annika? She's a tougher sell. You should know she's the brains of that outfit." Volkov chuckled. "She lets him think her ideas are his."

"Yeah, I picked up on that. She pulls his strings."

"The trouble with the younger ones like Arkady and Annika is that they were born here in the U.S. They don't know what it means to struggle. To them, going without their iPhones for a day is a major disaster. Back in Russia, you never knew when a friend would turn you in for some petty infraction just to get ahead. You could end up in prison for an off-hand comment ... even spoken in jest."

Mikels sensed he was in for another long rant about Volkov's early days in Russia. But he'd learned that the less he said the better, so he remained attentive.

Volkov continued reminiscing. "Here, we call it the FBI. In Russia, it's the Federal Security Service—formerly the KGB. I know. I was one of them. Power with no restraint is dangerous, Gregor. I saw my own demise coming, so I got out before it was too late."

"You mean, before 'poof'?"

"Yes." Volkov laughed. "You like 'poof,' huh?"

Sharing the laugh, Mikels quipped, "Yeah, as long as it doesn't apply to me."

Volkov stood up, and they shook hands. He said, "Welcome to our Russo-American family, Gregor Mikhailovich."

"Thank you, Yuri Volkovich. I knew you would understand."

The two newly minted compatriots sauntered downhill toward the waterline. Volkov picked up several stones and skimmed them out over the water. He asked, "What are your dreams, Gregor? Everyone has dreams ... goals. What are you aiming at in life?"

"Funny you should ask." Mikels reached into his jacket pocket and pulled out the brochure. "I'd like your opinion on something, Yuri. Ever hear of Regal yachts?"

Volkov examined the brochure and said, "That's not a yacht, that's a boat. Someday I'll show you a real yacht."

CHAPTER 33

Stroudsburg, Pennsylvania Police Department.

"BOB, I HAVE news." Eric Sullivan half-sat on the detective's desk during the call. "Caleb dumped my truck in the parking lot of the Stroudsburg PD parking lot. Some balls, huh? Oh, by the way, he left a smartass note written on an envelope. It said, 'Please, forgive me, Eric.' I say 'smartass' because we've been discussing forgiveness ... his old man taking off and all that."

"Uh-huh." Bob, thinking out loud, said, "He must have picked up something else. It's not like him to break into someone's car and steal it. Is there a car rental agency nearby?"

"Way ahead of ya, Sarge. Two blocks down, he rented a white Dodge minivan from Enterprise. I think he's goin' for his girlfriend."

"No doubt. Between Nezzie and Worten, he learned she's in an abandoned school building in Brooklyn. He's smart. He'll figure it out, narrow it down. All he needs to do is go online. Mack and I are heading over to Brooklyn to check it out."

Eric said apologetically, "There's more, Bob, and it's not so good. My little .38 Chief's Special Air Weight was under the front seat of my truck. I didn't think of it when last we spoke."

"Uh-oh. Is that the piece you used to finish off the second guy?"

"What? How did you—"

"Oh, c'mon, Eric. You didn't think that went unnoticed, did ya?"

"Well, I did wonder why the forensic boys didn't pick up on it … the difference in caliber, ya know?"

"Yeah, well, they did. In spite of the rules, we all carried a backup piece in those years. Better to be tried by twelve than carried by six, right? Besides, you were the hero, taking out those two mokes. We couldn't allow your image to be tarnished by a small breach of protocol. We doctored the reports to show you reloaded your service weapon—less those two shots, of course."

"Without that little gun, Sarge, I'd be dead. After shattering my knee, he was moving in for the kill. I was so lucky. Have you ever tried to hit something with a two-incher?"

"Sometimes luck is all we have. Gotta go now. I'll let you know what happens."

"Good luck!"

Following a circuitous route along the backroads of eastern Pennsylvania, Caleb took a chance on main roads and stopped at the Enterprise office in Lehigh Valley International Airport just outside Allentown. He complained about a knocking noise in his rental van. In just twenty minutes, he was switched to another minivan—dark green this time. He thought, *I might as well give them a run for their money.*

Crossing the Delaware River at Easton, he picked up Interstate 78 eastbound through New Jersey. He stopped at the North Branch of the Hunterdon County Library in Clinton to research what he'd been told by Nezzie and Worten. The young woman in the reference section was helpful and set him up on a public computer. He Googled "abandoned schools in Brooklyn" and found three. He reversed their addresses and found one on Clarkson Avenue that had a business listed. It showed promise.

Spasibo ... isn't that Russian? I'm on my way, Jelly!

CHAPTER 34

ROSAMIE WOKE ANGEL, saying, "You come now. Missy Annika say you go to beach with babies. See Russia man, I think." The little seamstress was stressed. "You come fast, I think."

Angel was energized. She leaped from her bunk and began collecting the few possessions she was allowed: toiletries, three sets of underwear, and the clothes she wore when captured. She snatched her pillow up and put an index finger to her pursed lips. "I like this pillow. Please don't say anything if I take it."

Rosamie shrugged and said, "You take. Here, I give you more clothes. You wear at Bri-Beach, I think." She smiled. "You bery pretty in my clothes, Missy Ange."

Angel accepted the carefully folded bundle of clothing gratefully. "I won't forget this, Rosamie. I think we understand each other now."

"Yes. Unestan more better now. You go have good life, I think." The little seamstress hesitated awkwardly but compelled herself to reach for and hug Angel before leaving abruptly.

Angel spun herself around in a happy dizzying swirl, holding the pillow close. When she squeezed hard, the cell phone could be felt, but not when handled normally.

In a little while, I'll get to see Alicia and the others. All I have to do is convince Volkov my services can also be useful with the kids. Piece-a-cake!

When the twins arrived, she was grateful for the added bulk provided by Rosamie's clothing contribution. Bundling it all together concealed the pillow and phone from suspicious eyes. Walking down the hall took them past the window. She asked Vadim if she could stop for just a moment. She gazed out "her" window and sighed. Even though the screws were loose, no one could tell that just by looking. She thought, *Mr. Lock and Mr. Fire Escape Ladder, you guys were tough. I won't miss either of ya.*

Haughtily, Angel said, "Let's go, you guys. I've got an appointment with Mr. Volkov. And you know he gets what he wants ... and he won't like it if we're late."

The twins gave each other a puzzled look and took Angel to the basement garage where a van was waiting.

From the van's rear seat, Angel gazed longingly at the apartment buildings and small shops along Bedford Avenue. At mid-morning, Brooklyn's sidewalks and streets bustled with foot and vehicular traffic. It had been over a week since she was taken, and except for her catwalk sojourns, this was the first time she'd experienced anything outside her confinement. Seeing vibrant street life going on all around her was mesmerizing. Sunshine on her arm was soothing. Her thoughts wandered. *If I get out of this in one piece, I'll have a whole different outlook on life. I already do. I'm not who I was. I'm strong. I'm tough. I wonder what Caleb will think of me. Was I that dependent on him? Will he love the new me?*

Her reverie was violently interrupted. Vadim slammed on the brakes at Avenue U when a police car squealed to a stop in the intersection, its lights flashing and siren blaring. Ilia's right hand automatically flew beneath his jacket and into his left armpit. He shot a threatening look at Angel and warned, "Don't try anything. Both you and the cops will go down if you do."

Once a screaming fire engine cleared the intersection, the police car left, and they were allowed to proceed. Angel's snide answer confused the twins. "Don't worry. I ain't goin' nowhere. Anyway, I might like my new position."

As they drove on, Ilia frowned. He couldn't resist saying, "You're a strange one. We grab you and keep you locked up, and suddenly, you don't want your freedom? What's up with that?"

Angel responded haughtily, "Mind your own business. I'll let you know when I want to bail." She smiled coyly. "Or maybe I won't."

"That's no answer."

Angel's wicked expression conveyed a not-so-veiled threat. "Maybe you'd like to ask Mr. Volkov about my status?" Thrilled with her confidence, she thought, *Oh, I just love the new me!*

Ilia made a sour face and turned his attention to the surrounding traffic.

"I thought so," said Angel. She smiled triumphantly throughout the remainder of the short ride to Brighton Beach.

As they came to a stop in the rear yard of Volkov's mansion, Angel gazed out the window, appearing awestruck. "Wow, fabulous. Now this is me!"

She impatiently tore at the door handle and erupted from the van. She took in American Dacha by the Sea's ambient surroundings. With arms outstretched, she spun around, shouting exuberantly, "Take me home, Daddy!"

The twins eyed each other quizzically. Vadim shrugged. Ilia shook his head in wonder and said, "She's crazy … a nut job. Volkov can have her."

Following the twins up the walk, Angel concealed a smirk. *Yeah, I'm crazy. Crazy like a fox, you idiots. I'm just practicing. You'll all be off-balance before I'm done here.*

An hour later, Angel stood in the doorway of Volkov's study, admiring its luxurious trappings. She stepped over the threshold onto the marble tile, its semi-reflective surface shimmering the rays of the mid-day sun and radiating a soft golden glow. The exquisite Queen Victoria Jubilee pool table with its carved wooden inlay caught her eye first. Heavy Ankara drapes teased access to a saltwater swimming pool past the French doors leading to a patio beyond. A mauve Benetti's Ferrara sectional sofa faced a wall-to-wall fireplace with an imported coral surround. The ceiling was inlaid with a huge intricate carving of "Barge Haulers on the Volga."

Angel thought, *A bit overdone. The guy who lives here wants you to know he's important. Good to know.*

Yuri Volkov, wearing a richly embroidered, maroon smoking jacket, was comfortably ensconced in his oxblood Pollaro leather and oak armchair, sipping his usual Remy XO. He rose and smiled when he saw Angel.

Angel spoke first. "You have a magnificent home, Mr. Volkov."

"It's Yuri to you, Angel. I hope you will enjoy your stay here."

With a show of self-assurance, she answered, "Oh, I'm sure I will … Yuri."

As he guided her to the sectional, Volkov eyed Angel carefully. He said, "You seem different from your last visit. More alert. More … I don't know … more alive, I guess."

Responding with measured distaste and wearing a face-pout, she said, "Last time I was here, I was drugged by those two creeps in Brooklyn. Drugged—while their twin goons held me down." She looked around the room and added pleasantly, "As if I wouldn't want to come here on my own." Angel flowed smoothly down into the cushy sectional and, with an ever-so-slight wiggle, encouraged it to embrace her. She smiled warmly at Volkov.

Caught off-guard by Angel's laidback manner, Volkov blinked several times. He chose his words carefully. "I thought something was wrong then. I suppose you don't remember much from that visit."

Affecting a coquettish air, Angel lifted one eyebrow and answered, "Well, I do recall the finer points."

Volkov felt his heart rate increase. He sat down beside her, casually crossed his legs, and said, "Perhaps we could pick up where we left off. I would very much like that."

"And just where was that, Yuri?"

"You fell off into slumberland at what I would call a 'crucial moment,' if you get my meaning. It sort of confused me." Volkov gently placed his hand on Angel's knee.

"You are being nice. What you mean is, I passed out." Exercising control and intending to joust a bit with Volkov, Angel rose slowly, allowing his hand to slowly slide away. She meandered over to the pool table. Slowly dragging one finger along its inlaid edge, she stopped and rolled the cue ball around in her hand. She turned back to Volkov and asked, "May I?"

Wearing a patient smile, Volkov stiffly rose. "Of course." Intimating a double entendre, he said, "Shall we play?" He tightened the triangle of balls and chose two sticks from the cue rack and asked, "Would you like to break?"

Angel grinned confidently. *Sucka! I grew up with a pool cue in my hand. In my other life, what I couldn't make one way, I won on pool tables or shooting craps.*

Twenty minutes later, Volkov stood scratching his head. "Phew. I've never taken a beating like that before … and on my own table."

Angel asked, "Could it be that no one else would dare beat you ... on your own table or not? Fear changes people. It makes them weak. Haven't you noticed?"

Volkov stared at Angel for a long moment and said, "Something is going on here. How is it that *you* aren't concerned about beating me?" He frowned. "You seem to be able to say things to me others wouldn't dare. Why am I putting up with what would be insolence from someone else?"

Angel pouted and said, "It's just my way, I guess. If I offend, I'm sorry."

"No apology necessary." Volkov leaned both hands on the table. He marveled at her aplomb. "To be perfectly honest, I like it. It's refreshing. Especially coming from someone so ... so beautiful."

Angel shrugged. Sidestepping the flirtation, she said, "You know, Yuri, it isn't a bad thing to be disagreed with. We can all learn from one another."

"You mean something like considering other people's views?"

"Uh-huh."

"Maybe for some, but not for me. In Russia, we say, 'When you allow latitude, you get latitude.' No, my dear, tight control leads to the desired results."

Angel mused, "It must be lonely … I mean, having no one to share thoughts with."

Volkov shrugged. "It comes with the territory."

Angel frowned. "So sad."

Volkov, obviously uncomfortable with the direction of this conversation, changed the subject. "Well now, you've just arrived. Have you seen your room yet?"

"Yes, it's lovely. I dropped my things there and asked your maid to bring me right to you."

"Then why don't you go and freshen up? We can meet on the patio for lunch and talk some more."

On her way out, Angel threw a coy look over her shoulder and said, "Until later?"

Her playful comeback stirred Volkov. With a half-smile, he bowed his head slightly as she retreated from the study.

Angel sneered, *What a pompous, conceited ass! I wasn't sure how to handle you, but now I know. It's all about you—all the time. I can deal with that.*

Upon entering her room, Angel went directly to the faceplate of the air conditioner vent next to the bed and unscrewed it with a coin. Retrieving the cell phone, she sent a text to Mikels.

It said, "At the beach. In with V. lousy pool player. Will let you know about kids soon."

CHAPTER 35

Office of Chief of County Detectives,
Elizabeth, New Jersey.

CHIEF WORTEN'S OFFICE meeting comprised of Greg Mikels and Rafael Rivera, who was an investigator from the Brooklyn District Attorney's Office—plus Mack and Bob, who were in their vans on speakerphones.

Worten began, "Of all the issues facing us in this case, having Caleb loose and running around with a loaded handgun is the most pressing. We believe he's headed for Spasibo to rescue Angel. Let's have some ideas."

Mikels said, "We can't be too obvious around Spasibo or it'll blow the whole thing up. And it could get Angel hurt."

DA Investigator Rivera agreed. "I'd like to say our office could put extra eyes on the place, but we have so many out with Covid, we just don't have the manpower." He shifted uncomfortably in his chair and said, "There's another issue, difficult as it is to mention. How can we know anything we do at our end won't get back to the other side? I hate to say it, but when politicians get involved in police business, we all know what happens: Loose lips and sunken ships."

Mack spoke up, "I know we're not law enforcement, but we can spot Caleb, which is a plus. We're on the Belt Parkway ... almost there now. We'll set up in the neighborhood, and if he shows, we'll grab him before he gets into trouble."

Worten looked around the table. Hearing no dissenters, he said, "Sounds good. Keep us advised. Now, moving on to the legal aspects, I'd like to approach a judge for permission to install a wire in Volkov's home. Rafael, do you think you could handle that? It's in your jurisdiction."

"Absolutely, Chief. All we need are affidavits from Mikels and Angel to show probable cause, and—"

Mikels interrupted, "Hold it. That's not a problem for me, but it's very risky for Angel. Our time together has been counted in short minutes, often with bad guys present." He turned to Worten and said, "How about an affidavit from Mack regarding the beginnings of this, including the kidnapping of Angel? Even Caleb could sign one when we get him under control. Wouldn't that be enough to get a warrant for the bug?"

Rafael Rivera thought a moment and said, "I think so, but it will have to be cleared by my boss before we talk to a judge."

Frustrated, Worten said, "Look, we can't allow protocol to stand in the way. We have to move this along. Things are happening on the ground faster than we can keep up. Screw all that red tape. I'll have our prosecutor contact your district attorney and get this put on a fast track to a judge. How 'bout that?"

Bob chimed in grudgingly, "I hate to be the bugaboo in the bunch, but has anybody thought of the feds and their role? This is all heading toward their bailiwick. We all know that if there's any glory in it, they'll jump in to claim it. So shouldn't someone at least keep them up to speed?" He added comically, "Or maybe half-speed and staying the hell out of the way!"

Everyone laughed.

Chief Worten fielded that one. "I'll spoon-feed them. As long as this looks like a small-time police raid, they won't be interested. They won't get in our way."

Mikels said, "Once we get the court order for the bug, I can plant them, but we need someone to monitor and record them. Any thoughts on that?"

"We can help out on that, too," said Mack. "We're gonna be in the neighborhood anyway."

The meeting broke up with everyone agreeing to get Caleb under control, then go for the listening devices. Scraping chairs protested as the group rose from the table.

Worten bellowed over the group's parting small talk with, "We meet back here tomorrow! I'll keep everyone up to speed with email."

CHAPTER 36

FORMER KGB COLONEL Yuri Volkov was not used to waiting for others. He was becoming impatient. When asked if he needed anything else, Volkov dismissed his steward with a discourteous hand flick. Aimlessly running a finger around the rim of his glass, he pondered his soon-to-be liaison with Angel. He gazed out over his familiar bay view and spotted a sea bird skimming close to the water's surface, as if tempting the waves. The scene became a metaphor for his favorite Batyushkov poem: *I am the depth of the sea; she is the temptress in flight. The strength of my will shall bring her to me.*

He pouted. Part of him was the calm, calculating commander, accepting nothing less than he demanded. But there was another side to him today … something disconcerting.

How is it I feel like a schoolboy anticipating his first time with a woman? What is it about her that is so different from others? Why don't I feel in control when I'm with her?

The conundrum resolved itself. *Like the sea bird, she skims the waves over me ... just beyond reach. She keeps me off balance. She controls conversations. She's not afraid of me and says what she thinks. I'm too used to idiots fawning all over me ... hypocritical, disingenuous idiots. Not her. She is who she is and without reservation. She's captivating!*

Volkov chided himself for periodically glancing at the French doors. *She'll be here soon enough. Don't appear anxious, you old fool.*

She knew what was about to come. She would have sex with Volkov. Not only was it demanded, but it was also expected. It was why she was here in Brighton Beach. It was unavoidable. She knew she could handle the aftermath ... the guilt, the shame. She could handle it because there was no alternative to saving Alicia and the other children from being sold to sick, sexual deviates.

Before pushing open the French doors, she took a deep breath. Through the curtains, she caught a glimpse of Volkov looking out at the water ... waiting for her. She thought hatefully, *I am resurrecting my past life and inflicting it on you, you bastard. You may think you're a big shot, but like all self-indulgent fools, you're nothing. In the end, I will break you.*

Even in the act of rising, Colonel Volkov admonished himself. *I don't stand up for anyone. Why do I mindlessly do it for her?*

"Well, that didn't take long." Ceremoniously waving his hand in a semi-circle, he proclaimed, "Welcome to my ocean view."

During lunch, Angel monopolized their tête-à-tête. Most of their discussions were peripheral. Angel's status—her real purpose for being there—was not brought up. Not at first. First, there would be verbal foreplay.

Angel queried, "Yuri, may I ask a personal question?"

"It depends. How personal?"

Angel laughed. "It's just that your English is so perfect. I've met many people from other countries, and I can always pick up a slight accent. Not with you. Why is that?"

"My dear, English—including its American slang—was drilled into all KGB foreign operatives. If you couldn't master American-style English, you were out."

"Hmph, I've heard about the KGB, but I suppose that's our American propaganda."

"Hah, you are so naïve. Both sides are adept in the use of propaganda. It's a form of warfare. Deploying the influence of thought can be very effective. Imagine winning a war without firing a shot."

"Manipulating thoughts—mind control. How treacherous!" Angel's voice perked up. With her hands up in mock surrender, she proclaimed, "The thought police ... what a world!"

Volkov responded, "You're pretty good at orchestrating thoughts yourself, Angel."

It's now or never, she thought. "Do you think so, Yuri?" She tilted her head, and, with a half-smile, raised her left eyebrow. She asked, "What am I thinking right now?" *C'mon, you old fart. Take the bait.*

Volkov grinned slyly and said, "If I'm guessing right, I think we are sharing the same thought ... and don't you suppose it's time we stopped thinking and did something about it?" *Little sea bird, my waves are tempting you now!*

She met his grin with her own. "Oh, absolutely. Lead on, my colonel." Walking behind and unseen by him, Angel's smile drained ... knowing what was to come.

Volkov was overwhelmed with Batyushkov: *I am the sea; she is the temptress— Soon, my little bird ... soon.*

As they went through the French doors, Angel tried to think positively. She mused, *Help is coming soon, Alicia ... soon.*

CHAPTER 37

Clarkson Avenue, Brooklyn.

CALEB'S CONCENTRATION WAS under assault. The narrow neighborhood streets were brimming with frenetic activity. Impatient drivers jockeyed for position with their horns blaring.

Turning buses seemed too big for the road, and wobbling, over-confident bicyclists avoided certain death by inches.

He thought, *The noise, the traffic ... how can anyone live here? How does anything normal come out of this chaos?* The serenity of Sullivan's cabin in the woods stood in sharp contrast to this hectic metropolitan environment.

During his hours-long road trip from Pennsylvania's tranquil mountains and lakes, he'd struggled with what he would do when he found the people holding Angel. His thoughts ranged from simply barging in and taking her to cautiously waiting and scoping out the place.

I'll walk in and confront the first one I see. I'll point Eric's gun at them and demand to see Angel. Then I'll grab her, and we'll get out. Maybe I'll shoot a couple of times into the ceiling to scare them. Or ... maybe I should watch the place for a while and look for an opportunity to sneak her out.

Indecisive and anxious, he summed it up with, *I'll figure it out when I get there.*

Caleb was running on emotion. He was about to enter a dangerous, unfamiliar world, and he knew it. In his mind, he had no choice but to go forward ... no matter what. He owed it to Angel. *I got her into this mess; it's my job to get her out.*

Having located the old school on Clarkson Avenue, he began looking for a parking space. It took three tedious trips around the block before he found a spot, only one-hundred feet from Spasibo's front door. Caleb sat for a moment, gathering himself.

"This is it," he announced calmly. Alighting from the minivan, Caleb set out at a determined stride, his right hand jammed in his pocket, holding the small .38 Special tightly. *I'm coming, Angel.*

As he walked past an alley opening, he was seized from behind on either side by powerful hands, jerked out of public view, and lugged into the narrow passageway. He was pushed face-down into years of accumulated alley debris. A hand gripped the nape of his neck, while a knee settled into the small of this back, pinning him firmly. Stunned, he struggled, but they were too strong. His heart rate soared. He couldn't breathe. The pain. It flooded back to him: *The porch, my camera card, black sneakers, Angel ... NO!*

A deep voice asked, "What should we do with him?"

"We could ask inside, but we know the answer."

"Ya think? Maybe he should be put with the others on the Staten Island side."

"Yeah. First, let's rough him up a little."

Caleb was terrified. He stuttered, "N-n-no. Wait, I can explain. I—"

Strong hands reached down and flipped him over onto his back. Caleb tensed; his eyes tightly closed. He scrunched his face and raised his hands defensively. He waited for the worst. After a few seconds passed and no blows came, he peeked through splayed out fingers.

Astonished, he said, "You! How did you—"

Mack and Bob stood over him, snickering.

Bob teased, "Expecting black sneakers, were ya?"

Mack said, "You stupid little jerk. You almost blew this whole thing. And you could have gotten Angel killed." He yanked Caleb to his feet.

Bob added, "She's not even in there, you idiot."

They pulled Caleb farther into the alley. Mack grabbed Caleb's hair and yanked his head back. "Ya see way up there? See that third-floor window? That's where your girlfriend crawled out, went up that sorry ass lookin' fire escape ladder to the fourth floor, and found a bunch of scared kids … kids waiting to be sold to sex perverts. Right now, she's risking everything to save those kids, and you're not gonna mess it up. Got it, cowboy?"

Mack relaxed his grip.

Caleb continued to gaze up at the fire escape. He meekly said, "She went … up there?"

"She did. And she is still in danger … her choice. Not yours, not mine, not your Uncle Bill's. She's a terrifically brave girl, and, despite you, we are going to do this right for her and those children."

Still incredulous, Caleb said, "I can't believe it. It's just not like her. She doesn't have … she's not that, uh, strong."

Bob said, "You'd better get used to the idea, buster. She's more than you—and a lot of other people—give her credit for."

Caleb wiped the alley's grime from his chin and brushed off his clothes. Nodding his head subserviently, he quietly said, "How can I help?"

Mack said, "That's more like it. You will do just what we say. First, we find an Enterprise store and get rid of your van. Then we'll take a day at the beach."

Bob added, "Yeah, we have a rendezvous with some Ruskies."
Mack held out his opened palm to Caleb, wiggled his fingers, and
said, "Gimme."

Caleb reluctantly turned over Eric Sullivan's prized possession—the old backup piece that had saved one life and nearly
gotten another into deep trouble.

CHAPTER 38

Volkov's "American Dacha by the Sea"
three hours later that afternoon.

CAMILA HEADED THROUGH the study, opened the French
doors, and walked out onto the patio where Volkov and Angel
were sunning themselves. With a hint of scorn in her tone, she
said, "That lieutenant is here to see you again, Mr. Volkov."
She eyed Angel's skimpy swimsuit contemptuously and quickly
gazed skyward, finding the setting too unseemly for her liking.

"Camila, you will refer to our friend as 'Gregor.' He is one
of us, so kindly treat him accordingly."

Camilla dutifully responded, "Of course, sir. I will see him
in." But Angel picked up on her sour face as the nurse turned
and retreated through the French doors.

Volkov lifted his dark sunglasses and commented to Angel, "Now there, you see? You can tell she doesn't like Gregor, yet she bows to my instructions. No latitude, just obedience."

"Yes. But you don't know what else she is thinking, do you? You don't know what's behind her obvious dislike for him. That might be important someday."

"You would have to know Camila better to understand. She doesn't like any kind of policeman. Back in the USSR, she was tortured to give up information ... information she did not have. They nearly killed her. Using more civilized means, I determined she was innocent and put a stop to her suffering. I saw potential in her. She has been my loyal assistant ever since. She handles my business minutiae, and puts her nursing skills to work too."

Angel shrugged and said, "That only proves you do have a kinder, gentler side, my colonel."

Not entirely comfortable with Angel's assessment of him, all Volkov could say was, "Hmph!"

But this was new information. Angel realized she should be viewing Camila as more than just a nursemaid to the kids. She mused, *Loyal assistant? Business minutiae? I can just imagine what she knows about this whole operation.*

Mikels arrived and pulled a chair over. He nodded to Angel, trying hard not to look upon her near-nakedness. Self-conscious, she briskly nodded, covered herself with a beach towel, and looked away. The setting, while awkward for both, suggested to Mikels that Angel had made "certain progress" with the Russian.

"I have a security issue to discuss with you, Yuri." Mikels's eyes alternated from Volkov to Angel and back. "Is it, uh, okay to speak?"

Annoyed by the interruption, and more interested in Angel than Mikels's news, the Russian answered impatiently, "On security issues, yes. So … let's have it."

Mikels said, "I wondered if you've ever considered doing an electronic sweep of your place. A man in your position should be careful."

Volkov frowned and questioned, "Is there a reason for me to be alarmed?" He smiled at Angel and stroked her forearm.

Ignoring Volkov's cue that said, "Get lost—I'm busy," Mikels pushed harder. "Frankly, we don't know, do we? If you've never checked, you really don't know."

Volkov turned over, stiffened, and tightened his jaw. "What causes you to bring this up now?"

"Before I went on the Linden PD, and while in the army, I was in the intelligence service. We had debugging gear and routinely checked all vital installations: meeting rooms, field grade officers' quarters, and whenever dignitaries were expected. It's just good security."

Volkov thoughtfully tugged at a loose string on his bathing suit. After a moment, he granted Mikels the point. "It may be overly cautious, but what do we have to lose? Okay, set it up."

"I will. How about tomorrow? I'll stop by with equipment, and we'll do a sweep for electronic bugs. It'll only take an hour or so." Mikels stared hard at Angel. She returned with a quizzical look that smoothly dissolved into a concealed half-smile as she looked away.

She got it! Smart girl.

Volkov nodded his agreement and turned his attention back to Angel, dismissively waving Mikels off.

Mikels smugly grinned and winked at Angel behind Volkov's back. He made a T shape with his hands, indicating he would text her. As he rose to leave, Angel acknowledged his wink with the best she could offer—one slow, understanding blink.

As Mikels drove from American Dacha by the Sea, he shook his head in disbelief. He said aloud, "Game on, Colonel Vulgar. You are being double-teamed now. What an arrogant creep!"

The next day, Mikels arrived at the dacha just before 2 p.m. as Volkov and Angel were finishing up lunch on the patio. He joined them at the patio table and placed an aluminum case containing debugging equipment under the table. During their initial small talk, Mikels reached underneath and placed a small, magnetized listening device between two struts toward the table's center, assuring maximum concealment.

Sliding the aluminum case onto his lap, Mikels said, "So, Yuri, I will be walking around the house with this device looking for electronic signals. It will pick up emissions from small calculators and other innocent sources, so there could be false positives. I may need you to open a drawer or cabinet. I'll let you know."

Again, Volkov seemed disinterested. Barely tolerant of Mikels's intrusion into his everyday life at American Dacha by the Sea, he rose from the table and said, "Just do it. I'll be in Camila's office down the hall if you need me."

When Volkov walked away, Angel remained, providing the two undercovers a rare opportunity to speak to one another.

Mikels whispered, "Quickly ... I just attached a bug under the table, and I'm gonna put another one in the study—probably under the end table near the door. Like I said in the text last night, try to get him talking about the kids or anything else we might be interested in when you're close to either of those spots."

Angel leaned out from the lawn chair and peeked into the study to be sure Volkov had not returned. She spoke quickly. "I will. Just so you know, I think Camila is more than a nurse to the kids. He calls her 'his loyal assistant.' She knows a lot. Maybe you can have her checked out."

Mikels nodded. He studied Angel closely. "You okay? He's not hurting you, is he?"

Angel answered, "Nah, nothing I can't handle. I've dealt with his kind before. I think he covers up an inferiority complex with a lot of bluster and tough guy stuff. If I stroke his ego, I'll be okay."

Mikels said nothing, but his doubtful expression hung in the air.

Angel sat back in her chair and said, "No, I can handle him. You just do what you gotta do. I'm gonna work on getting to the kids." Sensing Mikels still wasn't convinced, she shook her head and added, "Really, don't worry. You men ... you're such puritans. It's just sex. Nothing new."

CHAPTER 39

BRIGHTON BEACH WAS a far cry from the Brooklyn neighborhoods Caleb had struggled through the day before. Though locals considered it busy for the off-season, it was, nevertheless, more laid-back than Brooklyn. A local Krauzer's and a construction site provided adequate surveillance positions for both vans. Each had his assignment: Bob sat in his van with eyes on the dacha's driveway to log who came and went, while a block away, Caleb and Mack monitored two audio receivers which Mikels had dropped off the night before at their Best Western in Coney Island.

Mack radioed Bob, "Bugging reception is great. I can hear glasses tinkling ... probably one of the servants clearing off the patio table."

"Roger that. I have a clear shot of the driveway. No action yet."

Walking on the beach was one of Volkov's least desirable pastimes. He placed a high value on his privacy, but for him, that kind of privacy ended the second his feet hit the sand.

Volkov stopped short and griped, "Goddamn riparian rights. I can't even fence off my beach. Angel, we've walked far enough. Let's go back."

"But why? This is so liberating, so free, don't you think?" She pushed harder to show she cared. "Yuri, why would you want to keep yourself cooped up in that house all the time?"

With a sour expression, he answered, "I don't need people. Not that way. Mindless socializing isn't my thing." He scanned the beach uncomfortably. "Besides, it's risky. I bet Gregor wouldn't approve of me being out here in public unprotected."

Apologetically, Angel said, "I guess I wasn't thinking. You're probably right."

"There you go again, Angel. You don't agree because you're afraid of me. No … you speak up because you have a mind of your own, and you are unafraid to share it." He took her hand as they strolled back toward the dacha.

She said, "I guess that comes from my college days. You know, college is supposed to make you think for yourself." With that comment, she fell silent, troubled … as if in deep thought. It showed.

Volkov reacted. "What?"

"For a moment, I was back in those days. I was thinking about my studies, the swim team, my friends, and wondering what my future would be like." She walked to the water's edge and looked out over the ocean. With tears welling up, she murmured, "And here I am."

Volkov was touched. "Hey, none of that." He gently pulled her chin around and said, "The past is the past, Angel. A famous Russian poet, Fyodor Dostoevsky, said, 'Whether I am a trembling creature or whether I have the right.'"

"What does it mean?"

"It means when a person finally dares to do something they were frightened of or reluctant to do for a long time."

Angel froze. Ever since she was taken from Caleb that day on the porch, she had sensed something different ... something she couldn't put her finger on, something she hadn't been able to define until now.

She said, "Yuri, please repeat that."

He did.

Angel thought, *I was frightened for a long time, but I dared. It has taken my enemy to identify me—to define me to myself. My new self!*

"Oh, Yuri, that is so true." Angel buried her head in Volkov's chest and sobbed. The tears were real. They came easily.

Taken aback, Volkov pushed her away but held her shoulders. Searching her face, he demanded, "What's all this about?"

She marshaled that new inner force and put it to work. Freshly inspired, she saw an opening. She thought, *Now. Now is the time.*

"I failed them. I failed the children when I got messed up. I dropped out of the children studies program at Rutgers. I'm no good. I don't deserve being here with you." She hung her head and wept.

She snuck a quick peek up at Volkov to see if it was working. It was.

His facial expression pained, Volkov rationalized, "That's not fair. You're young. You have plenty of time to make things right." He paused.

Being the man of action he was, he said, "I have an idea." He called Camila on his cell and told her to meet them on the patio.

Holding Angel tightly as they walked, he said, "Don't worry. Let's talk when we get back."

At the patio table, Volkov revealed his idea. "Camila, you will include Angel in your handling of the young ones. She has training in dealing with children under stress and can help you keep them under control. As a practical matter, this should help you with those resistance problems that crop up from time to time. In the end, it should make your job easier."

Camila was shocked. Before she could protest, Volkov turned to Angel and said, "I think I can help you with your need to help children. But you must fully understand what is going on here. We take poor children from underdeveloped countries and match them up with wealthy people here and overseas. Their lives are, in the long run, enhanced. What they give up in return is nothing compared to their future potential."

Volkov turned back to Camila and said, "Angel will meet with you tomorrow morning. You two can decide how to work out the details." In his usual rude manner, he dismissed Camila, saying, "In the meantime, I will continue this with Angel ... alone."

Camila rose stiffly. While walking away, she said over her shoulder, "As you wish, sir." However, the look she threw at Angel held anything but good wishes.

Throughout the conversation, Angel remained expression-less, suppressing an eruption of joy building inside. *It's working!*

Volkov edged closer to her and reasoned, "You're an edu-cated, intelligent woman. I hope you can grasp the idea of giving up something for a greater good."

Volkov went on, "The short story is that these kids are paired with upper-crust people—and I won't kid you—for sexual purposes." Wiggling his hands raised over his head in mocked animation, he cried out, "Oh, how terrible … child abuse!"

Speaking earnestly, he continued, "But they aren't in as much danger here as they would be back in their home countries. Poverty, lack of medical attention, political turmoil … the list goes on. Angel, if you can get past the lesser evil to conquer the greater evil, you can do this. How about it?"

"I didn't know … I had no idea." *Oh my God … he thinks of himself as a humanitarian! Saving the children.*

"You should know, these children will be in the company of accomplished, wealthy people. Some are very famous. To be rewarded and cared for much better than they could ever expect in their home countries makes sex a small price to pay."

Angel tilted her head and said, "I guess you're right when it comes to that. The little seamstress, Rosamie, tried to tell me the children would have a better life. I didn't get it then. But who better than her to explain it? Did you know she lost three small children to Filipino terrorists?"

Volkov, appreciating Angel's logic, said, "There, see? That's exactly the point. So you will do it?"

Angel put on an optimistic air. "I will. Anything I can do to help the children, I'm in." She hugged him. "And thank you, Yuri." Angel was energized. *Anything is possible if you dare. Thank you too, Mr. Dostoevsky!*

"You're welcome, Angel." Ever the manipulator, Colonel Yuri Volkov had a parallel thought. *Thanks, Fyodor Dostoevsky, my friend. That was easy.*

CHAPTER 40

In the rear of Mack's van within sight of the Volkov house.

MACK YANKED HIS headphones off. "This bastard thinks he's saving kids. I can't believe I'm hearing this!"

Caleb sat staring at the recording device. In a subdued voice, he said, "You can't believe it? That's my Jelly in there, and I can't believe that. She's in the middle of a friggin' child sex-for-sale operation, and we just sit here? This is wrong. We should be doing something!"

Mack said, "We are, Caleb. What we're doing here, and what she's doing in there, will put these people away for a long time. It could also flush out a lot of big-shot sexual predators. Your girl is doing everything right. She's saving the kids and getting the evidence we need."

"I know, but—"

"There is no 'but'—it is what it is. Now don't make me regret bringing you along with us. You do anything stupid again, and I'll personally put you on ice … uncomfortable ice."

Squirming in his seat, Caleb said, "Okay, okay. It's just that … I guess I never really knew her."

"I wonder if she ever knew this side of herself."

Caleb stewed. "I wonder what she'll be like when this is over. I wonder what we'll be when it's over."

"Give it a chance, son. Life is full of changes, and most of them are good."

The next morning, the surveillance teams were in place again. All was quiet until 9:15 a.m.

Bob Higgins alerted Mack and Caleb. "Got a small white car coming out of the driveway. When they pass me, I can pick 'em up. Will let you know."

"Okay, Bob. We'll stay here." Mack thought it more important to monitor the receivers than to join Bob.

Bob reported, "Angel is the front seat passenger. The driver is a heavy-set woman. Might be Camila."

"Roger that."

"Hold on … they just pulled over. Looks like they're arguing." Less than a minute passed, and the car started back up.

228

Bob tailed the women for a little over a mile to an upscale neighborhood on East 9th Street. He radioed, "They pulled into what looks like a four-plex apartment building. They went in through the back, out of my sight. I'll sit here a while and see what shakes."

Mack queried, "Ya think it could be where the kids are being kept?"

"Could be. I don't know how many rooms there are altogether, but it's plenty big. Hey, Volkov told Camila to meet with Angel this morning, right? Wait … I just saw something … gotta move."

A minute later, Bob came back on the radio. "This is wild. The building backs up to a matching one on the next block. I caught a glimpse of them crossing backyards from one to the other. Yeah, for sure, there are plenty of rooms for twenty or so kids to be stashed. And there's a tall fence sealing off both back-yards. I think they're here, Mack."

Twenty minutes earlier.

Angel tried striking up a conversation with Camila as they left the dacha's driveway. She started out with small talk. "Another beautiful day at the beach, huh?"

Camila responded with a deprecating look. She said, "I have to put up with you … I don't have to like you, so shut your trap!"

"Oh … is that the way it is?"

"Uh-huh. You're in my world now, cutie pie. I'm in charge of prisoners in this army. And that's just what you are!" Emphasizing her point, Camila stepped hard on the gas and made a hard left turn, shoving Angel against her door.

Angel responded by backhanding Camila with a forceful shoulder slap. "Pull this fuckin' car over." She turned sideways in her seat and jabbed a fisted thumb sharply into that same shoulder. *I gotta get this under control now!*

Not expecting Angel's aggressive response, Camila reflexively braked hard and drew back, hitting her head against the driver's window. Stopped at the curb, their eyes met, hostility teeming.

Angel warned, "If you know what's good for you, you'll knock this off right now. I'm not the silly little piece of ass you think I am. I've been around too, sister, and you don't scare me. Do you wanna play ball, or would you rather explain to the man how you screwed up his plan?"

Camila broke eye contact first. She pulled back into traffic and calmly said, "We'll talk more about this when we get there."

"Yes, we will." Angel settled back and smirked. With an air of detached coolness, she said, "Then we can start over. We should get to know each other, Camila. After all, we're on the same team, right?"

"Hmph."

Angel chuckled. *I'm really getting to like the new me!*

CHAPTER 41

Dacha by the Sea

THE STEWARD POURED Mikels a cup of coffee, and said, "Mr. Volkov is on his way. He had to take an overseas call. You may wait here in the study."

"No problem." Mikels was tired. After a long duty shift, he'd no sooner arrived at his apartment close to 1 a.m. when Volkov called, demanding he come to Brighton Beach first thing in the morning.

Once the steward left the room, Mikels took the opportunity to swiftly confirm the bug was still under the small end table, then returned to his seat.

Volkov hustled into the study and sat across from Mikels in one of the Italian chairs. He seemed upbeat. "Gregor, my boy, thanks for coming over so early. I have some pressing things to discuss."

"Glad to be of help, Yuri." Mikels thought, *Whatever it is, Mack and Bob are recording this right now.*

Volkov said, "Let me get right down to business. First, I am putting you on a thousand-dollar-a-week salary. That is, with or without any assignments. When you do a job, you will be compensated extra for whatever that comes to. Sound okay?"

Smiling widely, Mikels said, "Sounds fantastic. Thanks, Yuri."

"I knew you'd like that." Yuri made a sour face and rang for the steward. "My coffee is cold." He glared at the servant. "Fix it."

Volkov sighed and turned back to Mikels. "Hard to get good help nowadays."

He got to the point. "Arkady tells me you are aware of our principal business here." He paused, waiting for a response.

"Yes." Mikels searched for the right words. "We provide special companionship to, uh, special people—" He hesitated. He was going to add to that but decided to let it hang out there.

"Right, but I want to fill you in more completely." As if sharing a secret, Volkov leaned forward with both elbows resting on his knees.

"We also take underprivileged children from backward countries and offer them opportunities they would never have back home. They are well compensated. Understand?"

"Understood. They end up better off."

"Exactly, but there is another market opening up, and I want in."

Mikels said quizzically, "I'm afraid you've lost me."

"Are you familiar with Jeffrey Epstein and Ghislaine Maxwell? The recently deceased Epstein ... and his girlfriend? You know ... the procurer?"

"Of course, who isn't?" Mikels gave the impression he was figuring it out with a brief pause. He said, "Ah, I get it. Do we see a business opportunity here? Are we going to fill the void created by Epstein's—shall we say—rude departure?"

Volkov chuckled, "You are a quick study, my boy. I knew you would understand. Now, here's the plan. I see the new girl, Angel, as perfect for what I have in mind. She and I talked yesterday. I immediately saw in her an opportunity to move forward with my new venture. Right now, Camila is introducing her to the younger foreign children we have ready for distribution. We'll see how well she does with them, and when the time is right, we'll use her to bring in American teenage girls needed for certain discerning clients."

The hair on Mikels's neck tingled. Struggling to maintain composure, he said, "Brilliant. Take a business model that works. She's young ... early twenties. She's good-looking and a perfect model for the teen set. Great idea, but—"

"What?"

"Epstein was in with high society, right? He had contacts and lots of years developing them. We don't have those contacts."

The Russian smiled confidently and said, "But you see, Gregor, I have contacts, myself. I've developed several high-flyers on Wall Street, a Hollywood producer, and one very special senator in contact with an even larger pool of potential clients. Soon, they'll all be in my pocket … all with that same perverted lifestyle."

"Beautiful!" Mikels wanted to vomit. *Discussing this as if it was a legitimate business deal is sickening!*

Self-assured, Volkov continued, "There is, however, a difference between me and Epstein. He dabbled in his own services. Just like a drug dealer who uses his own product, Epstein's habit eventually did him in. That's not me. I will be the invisible string-puller. The Wizard of Oz, if you will."

Mikels quipped, "Bad analogy … don't forget, he got caught behind his own curtain."

Volkov jokingly shot back, "But this curtain—unlike that old iron curtain—won't fold." They both laughed. Volkov went on in a more serious tone. "The reason we are here this morning is that I want you to monitor Angel's progress. I learned from Arkady that you get along well with her. Watch her. Talk to her. Get a feel for how well she would fit into my plan. In the meantime, I will be setting up connections in and around the city. Got it?"

"When do I start?" *And all this is on tape. Unbelievable!*

"Today," Volkov directed. "Go over to 1949 East 10th Street right here in Little Russia and meet with Camila. She already knows about this and can be of help to you."

"I'm on it, Boss."

CHAPTER 42

Mack's surveillance van

MACK AND CALEB sat in the van, staring at each other in disbelief.

"In my twenty-five years of investigations, I've never heard anything like that," Mack said.

Caleb asked, "What do we do now?"

"We call in, Caleb. Worten has to hear this right away." Mack rewound the tape. When Worten came on the phone, Mack switched to speakerphone and pushed play.

After leaving Brighton Beach, Mikels stopped at Spasibo to make peace with Arkady and Annika. It had been three days since he went over to Volkov—he had wanted to give the siblings a chance to cool down before facing them.

"So loyalty isn't your strong suit, is it?" Arkady said, twirling a pen, and slouched down behind his desk.

Mikels argued, "You have to understand, I need the money. Volkov pays well. More than you could hope to. Under the same circumstances, you would do the same."

Far from satisfied, Arkady said sarcastically, "So money trumps loyalty, right?"

"I suppose, but you should look at it this way—you now have a friend in Brighton Beach, not just a boss. A boss who, by the way, puts you down at every opportunity. I can let you know what's going on with Yuri. I'll keep you in the loop. I owe you that much. Don't you see? It'll be better than you had it before."

"What about the missing camera card? Does he know about that? Has Angel told him? Have you told him?"

"C'mon, man. If I told him about that, I'd be in as much trouble as you for not mentioning it earlier. And Angel? Hell, she's scared to death of Volkov. No worries there either."

Seemingly satisfied, Arkady changed the subject. "In the next couple of days, we will be receiving another shipment. You can tell your new boss everything is moving along smoothly.

This group is Asian, so he will need Rosamie to spend time at the beach when they transfer over."

"Rosamie? The seamstress?"

"Uh-huh. She's fluent in most eastern dialects, as well as Spanish. Filipinos have their own language. It's a hodge-podge of Spanish, Chinese, Japanese, and others." Arkady scoffed, "It's called—are you ready for this? 'Bamboo.'"

"Okay, I'll let Yuri know."

Arkady asked, "Speaking of Angel, how's she doing?"

"I don't see her much. Yuri keeps her stashed away, if you get my drift."

Arkady snickered knowingly and stepped over to his window. Pensively regarding the street traffic below, he said, "You've come a long way in a short time, Gregor. Be careful. The further up the ladder you go, the harder you fall."

"Tell me about it. I know. I never put a foot down without knowing what's under it, my friend." Mikels added to himself, *Don't I know it!*

With a grim expression, Arkady turned to face Mikels. "Yeah, landmines are everywhere, Gregor. You know Volkov ... 'poof!'"

On the phone with Chief Worten.

Hearing the tape left Chief Worten astonished. "That is the best-recorded evidence of criminal intent I've ever heard. Imagine the balls on this guy, thinking he can be the new Epstein."

Mack added, "And thinking he can pull strings in the background … incredible!"

"Uh-huh. Let's just keep going with this. Angel seems to be handling herself well, and Mikels has become a close confidant of Volkov. Could we ask for more?"

"I suppose not. But there must be an end game somewhere here. I don't think we can allow the children who are there now to be—I'll use their word— 'distributed,' do you?"

"No, that's for sure." The chief paused, then said, "Maybe there's a way we can delay them while we get more evidence. I'll think about that."

"You mean like a moving street surveillance when you want to control the other guy by putting one car ahead to slow him down?"

"Yup. Good analogy. I'll get back to you on that."

Mack looked across the van at Caleb and said, "Caleb says hello, Chief."

Worten ended the call with, "Tell him he should be proud of his girl."

Caleb spoke up, "I am, Uncle." He stared out of the van's one-way window and thought, *I wonder.*

CHAPTER 43

CAMILA AND ANGEL faced each other across a table in a small makeshift office in the dining room of the East 9th Street house. Their strained relationship still hung in the air since the incident in the car minutes earlier.

Camila sat stone-faced. She said impassively, "Okay, you wanted to talk."

Angel said, "You and I have a lot in common, Camila."

With a wry smile, Camila countered, "I don't think so."

"Oh, we do. We both were saved by men we owe our lives to. We feel deep loyalty to them, yet they go on with their games … their criminal games." Angel paused, looking into Camila's eyes. "How am I doing?"

Camila swallowed hard but tried to hold out against Angel's logic. "So … this is some kind of clever argument?"

"Yuri told me you were tortured. He said you were innocent, and he saved you."

Camila's tough exterior collapsed. In a subdued voice, she said, "The KGB are animals. They enjoy causing pain. Back in Russia, I was a trained nurse. I was assigned to care for an army major after they tortured him. He was accused of treason. I didn't even talk to him about anything, but they accused me of holding back information. I was terrified. The pain was—"

She couldn't go on. Hands folded in her lap, she sat stoically staring at the floor. Angel reached across and held her hand for a long moment.

"Okay, my turn. I fooled around with drugs. It got so bad I dropped out of college. One night, I got high and was passed around by a biker gang. I was so ashamed. When my parents found out, they threw me out. I lived on the streets that whole summer. I did what I had to do to survive. I fell deeper and deeper into drugs. I overdosed twice. The second time, Caleb found me on a curb … nearly dead. He took me to a hospital and waited until I could leave. He lied and said he was my brother and took me home. He got me detoxed. I owe him … big time."

All Camila could say was, "Sorry."

Angel said, "So you see? We do have a lot in common."

"I suppose so." Still not won over, Camila dug deeper. "How is it you are here? How did that happen?"

Angel was ready for the question. "I was on a modeling assignment, but it was a phony setup. I think it must have been a date rape drug that got me. Arkady's two goons—you know, the twins—they grabbed me. I spent a week in Brooklyn before Yuri got me out of there. So, you see, I owe him too."

"I see." Camila softened her attitude. "I was wrong about you. Let's start over."

They both smiled. Camila suggested they go across the yard and inspect the children.

As they crossed from one backyard to the other, Angel said, "I'm through being a victim, Camila. It just doesn't fit my idea of a future anymore."

Camila came back with, "I could learn from you, not the other way around."

Trying to tamp down excitement in her voice, Angel asked, "Do any of them speak English?" Her mind screamed, *I'm here, Alicia.*

"Mostly Spanish."

"What ages are they?"

"From what I can gather, between nine and fourteen or so. We don't have birth certificates here, ya know?"

Angel approached the subject carefully. "Not that I'm offended, but isn't that a little young? I mean … is there really a market for prepubescent kids?"

"You'd be surprised. Besides, girls are maturing much younger these days."

Angel followed Camila up the back steps of the East 10th Street address. As they drew closer, Angel could hear young voices in animated discussion, along with music and what sounded like computer games, but on steroids. It was loud. Anyone listening would think it was just a typical party full of spoiled kids having a good time.

They passed through a kitchen area, down a hallway, and into a large front room full of young children engaged in a variety of recreational activities. Angel scanned the room and picked out Alicia in seconds. When the girl spotted Angel, she jolted to attention and was about to run to her, but Angel frowned and rapidly shook her head. Alicia caught on. She grinned and returned to her computer game.

Angel remarked, "They seem happy. Do they know? I mean … do they understand where they are going?"

Camila answered, "In vague terms, yes. Your job will be to prepare them psychologically for their assignments."

"I see. A kind of brainwashing." Angel's disgust was hard to conceal.

"You could put it that way. I prefer 'training.' Brainwashing sounds too, uh … Soviet, no?" She laughed at her own attempt at humor.

Suddenly, Camila gently grabbed Angel's elbow and guided her into an adjoining room. She spoke in a subdued tone. "Look, I'm not supposed to tell you this." She paused. The look on her face showed she was struggling to decide whether to go on.

Angel frowned. "What is it?"

Camila made her decision. "You and I are grooming this bunch, but I'm supposed to be grooming you too."

"Grooming me? What for?"

"Yuri wants to move in on Epstein's circle, and he sees you as a means of bringing in girls the right age. The early to mid-teens; the ones who know enough about sex but don't have a lot of experience. There's lots of demand and big money out there."

"Wow." Angel thought fast. "Sounds like an opportunity for me."

"Uh-huh. It's a step up. You'll make money and have more freedom. Or you can go back to your old life. Which do you think has more of a future, Angel?"

"Are you kidding? No contest. Count me in!"

246

"That makes my job a lot easier. Just don't tell Yuri I told you, okay?"

"Sure. It'll be our secret." *This is getting creepy. Gotta let Greg know.*

CHAPTER 44

*Office of the Brooklyn District Attorney, 350
Jay Street, Brooklyn, New York.*

CHIEF WORTEN MET with Brooklyn DA Investigator Rafael
Rivera. They discussed the issue of the children being ready for
distribution.

Worten explained, "Our intelligence indicates they're gonna
begin selling off the children from Brighton Beach. We don't
know exactly when, but it presents a major problem for us. We're
hearing—thanks to your boss and the judge that issued the warrant for the bugs—really good evidence against Yuri Volkov. But
if we bust him prematurely, we'll miss getting his clients—the
real child abusers—off the streets. Describing them as 'end users'
turns my stomach."

Rivera was sympathetic. "I understand. What do you
have in mind?"

"Let's sit down with your boss. This is above our pay grades."
Rivera called upstairs, and an emergency meeting was arranged
with Brooklyn District Attorney Vance Hetfield.

*Later that afternoon at Senator Maxwell's address,
Williamsburg Section of Brooklyn, NY.*

Senator Maxwell Sturbridge greeted Worten and Rivera with
warm, lingering handshakes. He said, "I'm always happy to sit
down with law enforcement. What can I do for you today? Please,
come in and have a seat."

They stood. Rivera spoke first. "Senator, this is not a social
call. The Brooklyn DA sent me over to ask you to explain some
photos that were taken of you over in Jersey." He motioned
to Worten.

Worten said nothing. He pulled several blown-up photos out
of a folder and spread them out across a conference table nearby.

Senator Sturbridge drew closer, squinted at the photographs,
reached for his glasses, and looked back up at the investigators.
Momentarily caught off guard, his eyes revealing panic, Sturbridge incoherently mumbled something. Then, feigning outrage,
he demanded, "Where did you get these?"

Worten stepped closer and faced the senator down. "You
know perfectly well where they came from. And you know just
what they mean."

His indignant attitude demolished, Sturbridge staggered and crumpled into a chair. His breath coming in short pants, he murmured, "What now?"

Rivera answered, "This comes directly from the DA. You will give up your Senate seat immediately. You will not discuss this with anyone. You will cooperate with us by revealing all that you know about this sex ring. After that, a decision will be made about whether or not to charge you."

Digging deep and coming up with bogus courage, Sturbridge said, "You're bluffing. You know perfectly well there's not enough in those photographs to prosecute anyone. You forget, I was a criminal attorney before I went into politics." His voice breaking, he added, "Besides, the DA and I are in the same party. He wouldn't dare—"

Worten wasn't intimidated. He cut the senator off. "Maybe so, sir, but the court of public opinion doesn't follow the rules of evidence, does it? Your political career is over. You're the small fry on the merry-go-round in this case. Would you rather wait until someone else grabs the ring first? What you do from here on in determines the rest of your life."

Rivera ended the meeting with, "It's in your ballpark, Senator. Do the right thing."

The meeting lasted a little over two minutes. Senator Sturbridge was left slumped in his chair, his head in his hands.

Back in Rivera's detective car, Worten said, "We shook him up good."

"Yeah. The first thing he's gonna do is contact Volkov. That oughta put a crimp in their plans to distribute those kids for a while."

"Uh-huh. Keeping them off-balance is just what we want right now. Let's hope it works."

CHAPTER 45

LEANING AGAINST THE pool table, Volkov swished his Remy Martin around and condescendingly asked, "So what's the emergency, Maxwell? Why couldn't you speak on the phone?"

Senator Sturbridge paced back and forth. "Two investigators came to my office today and dropped these on me." His hands shook as he handed the photographs over to Volkov.

Volkov reviewed the photos. "Is this you? Is this your car?"

"My wife's. These were taken over in Jersey, last month, I think."

Yuri's frown deepened. "Is this what I think it is? Is that the twins with a little kid?"

Sturbridge looked away.

Volkov was livid. "You idiot. You've brought the law down on us, and the first thing you do is run to my house. Fool!"

"Yuri, I'm sorry, I never—"

"Shut up and let me think." *Could the police have taken the photos?*

Sturbridge whined, "Arkady did his best to get this under control, but—"

"Arkady? What does he have to do with this?"

Mack and Caleb got it all on tape.

Forty minutes later.

Bob radioed, "A fancy Mercedes just turned into Volkov's drive-way. He was in a hurry."

"Okay. We're ready, Bob."

Caleb readied his camera in anticipation of something else coming up. Mack nodded approvingly. "You might have a future in this business, Caleb."

Volkov met Arkady at the back door. It wasn't until they reached the study that their conversation was picked up by the listening device.

"I'm sorry, Yuri. We didn't want to upset you with what seemed trivial at the time."

In the van, Mack and Caleb locked eyes, listening attentively.

Volkov grilled Arkady, "You mean to tell me you thought incriminating photos of Senator Sturbridge could be trivial?"

Mack whispered, "That was Volkov." Caleb nodded.

Arkady whined, "Well, no. It wasn't like that. We didn't know what was in the photos, just that they may have existed. Believe me, we did our best to get them back, but—"

"But you didn't get them back. Worse, you failed to let me know about it. Now the cops are putting pressure on Sturbridge. He's frightened. He's weak. There's no telling where this could lead."

Caleb said, "What's that noise?" Mack shrugged.

Volkov stood at the pool table, violently slamming balls against its cushions so hard that several flew off the table. He tossed one of them up and down with one hand. Gritting his teeth, he threw the ball at Arkady and screamed, "You stupid asshole! Can you imagine what will happen if that little creep turns on us? Don't you see where this could lead?"

Arkady ducked the missile and whimpered, "What should we do?"

"You got us into this … you're gonna get us out. Send somebody to take care of him. I want Sturbridge gone today. Understand? Today!"

"You mean—"

"I mean remove him. I don't care how you do it. Just don't use those bumbling twins. I've had enough of their idiocy. And another thing, put everything on hold for now. No sales. No deals.

You hang onto the new ones, and we'll keep the group over on 10th until I get a better handle on this mess."

As Volkov stomped out onto the patio, he mumbled, "Gotta get Gregor on this right away."

In the van, Mack and Caleb stared wide-eyed at each other. They could hear the French doors slam. They heard Arkady cursing. "Fucking goddamn twins!"

CHAPTER 46

Senator Sturbridge's apartment, that evening.

"SO NOW YOU'RE back to threatening me again? It won't work. I've been a New York state senator for fifteen years, and I don't scare easily."

The small group stood in the front hallway of Sturbridge's Williamsburg multi-million-dollar apartment.

Worten smiled confidently and said, "Maybe this will put a limp in your swagger, Senator. This tape was made less than an hour after you left Brighton Beach today." He pushed play. Sturbridge backed up, pointing Rivera and Sturbridge toward the front parlor nearby as the little recorder came to life.

Though tinny on the small machine, the taped voices came across easily identifiable. He listened to Volkov sounding off at Arkady. When he heard Volkov order his murder, the senator's arrogance faded. He paled and began to shake.

"This can't be happening. He wouldn't dare." But when he searched Worten's face, his position crystalized. Reality was setting in.

He sighed and whispered, "I'm a dead man."

Rivera, playing good cop, said, "Not if we can help it, Senator. We have your home and office covered with special units. If and when anyone shows up, we'll be ready. In the meantime, you stay put."

"Bad cop" Worten took over. "Senator, I don't give a rat's ass about you. For all I care, Volkov can have you … dead or alive. But I do care about the kids you and others like you have been abusing. You are going to sit there, right now, and spill your guts. If you don't, we're out of here, and you're on your own."

Defeated, and only able to muster a hoarse whisper, Sturbridge said, "Okay, where do we start?"

"How about names, dates, and places?"

"What's the emergency, Yuri? I got here as fast as I could." Mikels grabbed a beer from the fridge in the study, popped it open, and joined Volkov at the patio table.

Volkov drummed his fingers on the tabletop impatiently. In a controlled but sinister voice, he said, "What the fuck is going on, Gregor? I learned that you and Arkady failed to recover a certain camera card that implicates a senator friend of mine. You come here as a friend, and you don't tell me? I have to squeeze it out of Arkady?"

Mikels had known what he was in for since Mack called him. He was ready for Volkov. Talking fast and with an indignant air, Mikels let loose. "Look, I'm just a small fish here. I follow orders. I did what I was told by Arkady, and I do the same for you. Do you think I would rat out Arkady to you? Would you expect me to rat you out to someone else?"

He recalled Mack saying, "Use the old 'best defense is a good offense' rule." Mikels continued, "Hey, I get enough drama and internal politics back at the PD, and I don't need it here too. Maybe you should find yourself another boy, Yuri," Mikels got up as if to leave, muttering, "This is bullshit!"

Going forward, Mikels had to be careful to avoid potential charges of entrapment. Knowing it was all on tape, whatever Volkov was about to say had to be voluntary. Any proposed actions had to be Volkov's idea.

Yuri raised his hands defensively, and with his head down, said, "Okay, okay. I get it. The fact is, I need you now more than ever."

Volkov explained that Senator Sturbridge was weak and could be turned by the police. He told Mikels that Sturbridge knew enough to implicate a lot of famous people in child sex trafficking. "I've insulated myself by staying in the background and putting deals together, so I'm not too worried about myself. But situations like this are bad for business. It makes us pull back for a while."

"How can I help?" Mikels asked.

"That's more like it. First, we have the problem of two groups that we need to hide somewhere. That's a total of thirty-five to forty kids worth a whole lot of money. Got any ideas?"

Mikels never even flinched. *You just said the magic words, Yuri. I hope the guys out there got all this on tape.* He answered, "Maybe. Let me think about it."

"I've taken some steps, and I may have the senator under control, but there's no telling what the cops may have figured out from their meeting with him."

"Wouldn't anything he says implicate himself too? I mean, after all this time, why would he roll over now?"

"It's that damn camera card Arkady couldn't get. Sturbridge is in several of the pictures."

Mikels acted taken aback, "Uh-oh. Not good."

Volkov explained, "He came here and blubbered all over himself. But that's not your problem. What I need from you is a place where we can safely store those two groups for a while."

"Yeah. I gotta make a call. Give me an hour or so."

"That's what I like about you, Gregor. You're a man of action … like me. You don't see an obstacle as a problem—more like a challenge to overcome. By the way, there's a good payday in this for you when you come through."

Mikels grinned widely. "That's what I like about you, Yuri. You appreciate talent."

As he left Volkov on the patio, Mikels thought, *Where the hell am I gonna find a place to store these kids? Or … maybe it's obvious.*

CHAPTER 47

CAMILA SAID, "WHY don't you look around? If you're gonna be helping me, you should also see if you can communicate with these kids. My Spanish is passable, but there are times I'm not so sure."

Angel said, "That's probably me too. I'll give it a try. Let me pick one out and see."

She returned to the front room and signaled Alicia to follow her. With more privacy in the kitchen, they were able to talk.

Alicia hugged Angel and cried, "Where were you? I worried."

Angel assured Alicia, "I'm here now, and I'll be here every day."

Over the next ten minutes, Angel got more details from Alicia. She learned Alicia was an orphan and forced to work for a vegetable farmer. She was sold to Honduran traffickers who gathered more children as they made their way toward the U.S. southern border. First, she rode on a bus; later, on a truck. She heard her captors negotiating bribes with local police each time they passed through a country's border or a regional checkpoint.

Angel was deeply moved by Alicia's story and promised to look after her, no matter what.

Then Camila interrupted. "I got a call from Yuri. He wants to see you now."

Angel caressed Alicia's hair and whispered, "I'll be back. Take care of the others."

Volkov was shooting pool when she entered the study. She said flippantly, "Look who's practicing. Should I be concerned?"

"Don't be a smartass. I don't keep you around to play pool with."

"Sorry, Yuri. I didn't mean—"

"It's okay. I'm having a bad day, and I need some company. Someone removed from all this crap I have to put up with." He smiled warmly. "Someone like you."

Volkov smelled of booze. She took his hand and said, "I'm here."

Yes … sit with me for a while." Volkov's speech was slurred.

"Sure, how can I help?"Volkov drained his Remi Martin and held it out to her. She refilled the glass and curled up next to him on the sofa. Alcohol-induced melancholy flowed as Volkov reminisced about his younger years in Russia.

"Back then, corruption was a way of life. Everyone was involved. The trick was to know your limits. If you were a young officer, you knew enough to leave the serious spoils to those above you. If you were a colonel in the KGB, the rules were the same. Putin and I played a game with the big shots in the Kremlin. The more we took, the more they got. Everybody was happy."

Angel, knowing all this was being recorded, encouraged Volkov to continue. "Interesting, but didn't anyone ever get caught and punished?"

"That's the best part. If you were thought to be disloyal, your crimes would be dredged up and used against you. If you toed the party line, you were safe. Corruption was elevated to professional heights. Those who knew how to play the game succeeded. Those who were greedy lost ... and usually disappeared." Laughing loudly, he added, "Poof!"

"Like a kind of balancing act, huh?"

"Exactly. Balancing. But then Putin made a mistake."

Over-emphasizing, he swung his drink around, spilling some on the carpet. "Oh yeah ... a big mistake. He took from the wrong pot, and it could have cost him big time. You see, it wasn't just how much you took—it was also important where you took it from. My friend, Vladimir, started draining funds from the military budget … from the same military budget that was falling behind America in the arms race. That was his mistake. As it happened, one of my duties was overseeing the military's auditing department. Vladimir's greed fell right into my lap."

Angel bent her knees and brought her feet up onto the sofa, affecting rapt fascination. "You discovered it. So what did you do?"

"I did what any good soldier would do. I covered it up. Doing so meant Putin owed me. He continued to rise in the party, and when he thought the time was right, he sent me to America to do my part."

Volkov smiled. "You see, while getting me out of Russia was a favor, at the same time, it removed a potential adversary at home. After all, I had enough on him to make him go 'poof.' But—always the schemer—he not only got me out of the way, but he also gained an experienced set of KGB eyes and ears on his enemy's soil. Smart man."

"So you know Vladimir Putin well. Wow." *Gotta keep him talking.*

Blinking several times in an effort to focus, Volkov answered, "Oh yeah. He set me up here with seed money, suggesting I take advantage of America's weak laws and help him out when he needed anything. It's been a good relationship. I live the American dream, and he rises to the top job in the Kremlin."

Volkov belched loudly and tried to get up. He stumbled. Angel steadied him and said, "My, Colonel, you are drunk! You need to sleep it off."

Volkov managed to nod his head, and, with Angel's help, he stumbled toward his bedroom.

As their voices faded beyond the reach of the electronic bugs, in the van 200 yards away, Mack rolled his eyes and said, "Jesus, this is a mess. Now we're up to our arses in Russian spies too. Gotta give Worten our daily report." He pulled his headset off and began punching in Worten's phone.

Caleb pushed his left hand harder against his earpiece and signaled to Mack that there was more.

Angel whispered into the patio tabletop, "I hope you are getting all this. He's out cold. I just took pictures of his calendar. It's all in Russian, but maybe it will help. I'll forward it to Mikels. Caleb, if you're listening, I love you. I'm going back to 10th Street with Alicia and the others. Please ask Mikels to stop in and see me, if he can. I'm so in the dark here. I've got to know what's goin' on outside. Camila says the kids are going soon. Thanks."

The van fell silent. Caleb sat staring, taking deep breaths, and swallowing hard.

Mack remarked, "What a woman. I can't believe how she's handling this." He reached over and finger-poked Caleb. "You are a lucky man."

CHAPTER 48

WORTEN, MIKELS, AND Rivera sat in the latter's office discussing the latest from Mack.

Rivera said, "I know the DA will want to bring in the FBI on this case once he hears that Putin came up on tape. No question."

Worten said, "Look, we are so close. We have enough to lock up Arkady, Annika, and Volkov for the rest of their lives. We even have a few dozen kidnapped children as evidence. With Senator Sturbridge spilling his guts, we'll be able to expose and possibly arrest others too. But bringing in the feds could drag this out forever. You both know damned well the FBI has always been the same. All they're interested in is image ... even at the expense of everybody else."

Mikels agreed but said, "First things first. Volkov gave me the job of putting the kids on ice. What if I did just that? We could take them out to Bob Higgins' friend in Pennsylvania, where they'll be safe. And once there are indictments in state court, the feds will be at a disadvantage 'cause they will need our evidence and—"

Worten finished it, "—and sealed grand jury evidence can't be released! Good thinking, Greg."

Mikels chuckled. "It's Gregor to you."

Rivera argued, "I don't want to piss on your parade, guys, but do you really think my district attorney will play along with this? Between you and me, he's much more likely to cave to the feds. He is a politician, you know."

Worten countered, "What if we give the spy angle to the feds, along with all those big shots Sturbridge is naming? Think of the positive press they'll get. They'll eat it up. Besides, you forget, Rafael, that this all started in Union County, New Jersey. Once my boss calls yours and says he will be indicting Arkady and Annika—beating Brooklyn to the punch—I'm pretty sure that politics, being the beast it is, will prevail. The Brooklyn District Attorney is not going to be upstaged by New Jersey. He'll play along with a joint venture … you'll see."

Rivera shrugged and said, "Point taken. There would be something in it for everyone. You're pretty good at politics yourself, Chief. Let's get this thing going!"

Bob called Eric Sullivan. "Mack got your little gun back, and Caleb is under control."

"Good news." Sullivan waited. "What else? There has to be something more from you."

"Yeah, well, there is. Very soon, you are going to have a school bus full of young children on your doorstep. Most speak no English and have been mentally abused for a couple of weeks. We need you to come up with a local camp or something out there to house and feed them until we can work out something more formal."

"Is that all? Would you like me to set up English classes too?"

"Yeah. That's all, wise guy."

"Ohhhhkaaay! Let me think … I have a friend with a camp. It's empty this season. Needs some work. The only glitch I can see is the cost of housing and food … maybe medicine, who knows?"

Bob thought a moment and said, "Costs might be covered with the money the bad guys have been paying our operative. It might not be that kosher, but a little creative accounting could make it work."

"I'll call you back, Sarge. Give me a little time."

"Thanks, pal. I knew I could count on you. See ya soon."

"Just one thing … see if you can get Caleb to come back. I'm not done with him yet."

"I'll check on that."

Mikels and Angel walked in the yard between the two houses on East 9th and 10th Streets. Camila had acted cool toward Mikels but directed him to the backyard when he arrived asking for Angel. He gestured back toward the house and asked, "What's with her? We've hardly met."

Angel said, "She's got cop issues."

"Who doesn't? Listen, I'm supposed to be working on you to go out and bring in teenage girls. The idea is to take up where Epstein left off. Believe that?"

"I know. Camila told me. But I need to know what's going on. When are the kids being shipped out? I'm more worried about that than anything else."

"It's all settled," said Mikels. "We'll be taking them to a camp in Pennsylvania, but Yuri won't know that. He'll be told I'm watching over them in upstate New York."

"Fantastic! When?" Angel was elated.

"As soon as I get back with Yuri and tell him it's set up."

"I guess you know by now that Yuri shot his mouth off about Putin. I was hoping they got that on tape."

"Uh-huh. They did, and that's where the FBI will come in. Not your worry."

Angel said, "I want to go with the kids."

"No can do! You'll have to stay here with Yuri until we're sure the grand jury has indicted them all. Then I'll get you out. It makes more sense to keep Yuri happy and preoccupied while we work out the legal details. Sorry."

"I guess, but please keep track of Alicia for me. I promised her she would be all right."

"Will do." Mikels tilted his head and said, "You know, you really are something else!"

"Yeah, I know." Angel laughed. "It's the new me."

CHAPTER 49

MIKELS SAT AT the patio table again, waiting for Volkov, but this time, it was different. He was joined by one of the twins. They sat uncomfortably, eyeing each other up. Mikels asked, "Which one are you?"

"Vadim. The boss tells me we are taking a little trip upstate with a load of kids."

This was a curveball, but Mikels reacted nonchalantly. "Really?"

Vadim frowned and said, "You got a problem with that?"

"Why would I? A little company on the way back will be good." Mikels wondered, *How do we handle this?*

Dripping wet, Volkov surprised them by coming up from the beach. Sitting in one of the lawn chairs, he began toweling off. He was all business. "I want to take some steps before things get out of control. We don't know if the senator shot his mouth off or not, so I want those kids out of here ASAP. Understood?"

Mikels and Vadim nodded their understanding.

"I've made arrangements with my contact near Wurtsboro. It's north about an hour-and-a-half. Your bus is parked on East 10th, waiting for you. You'll be met up there by my friend Boris." Volkov handed a note to Vadim. "You'll find the address and directions here. When you've delivered them, call me and come directly back." Without another word, he got up and went through the French doors into the study.

Mikels and Vadim exchanged blank looks and got up.

Mikels was conflicted. *Should I go along with this so I know where the children will be? Or should I blow the whistle on the whole bunch?*

He would receive his answer in a few short minutes. Vadim and Mikels drove the ten-minute ride to East 10th. As they approached, Mikels saw the empty charter bus at the curb. He thought, *Good, the children haven't boarded yet.*

Vadim parked and headed for the bus with Mikels close behind. Vadim began to board the bus but stopped abruptly.

The driver appeared from the second row of seats and seemed nervous. With eyes darting back and forth, he asked, "Uh … hello, are you the guy I'm supposed to report to?"

Vadim started to answer but stopped when he saw movement from the third and fourth rows.

The driver hurriedly leaped out of the way, jumping down into his driver's seat as Mack, Bob, and Caleb rushed forward and latched onto Vadim. Yelling for Mikels to lend a hand, they pulled the husky twin several feet down the aisle. Vadim was momentarily taken off balance, but he was stronger than his attackers and began to fight back.

Mikels's police instincts kicked in automatically. He stomped on the back of Vadim's right knee, resulting in the latter's momentary collapse in the aisle's close quarters. Though on the floor and on his side, the twin continued to struggle.

Caleb squeezed past Mack, leaned down, and shouted in Vadim's ear, "I see you wore your black sneakers today. Here's a taste of your own medicine, asshole!"

Caleb slammed a tire iron into Vadim's skull.

He was setting up to deliver another blow when Bob grabbed his arm and yelled, "He's down and out. We don't need to kill him, Caleb."

Mack turned to Mikels and breathlessly remarked, "We picked you up on the bug and decided to pull the plug. We cannot let these kids out of our control."

Taking a deep breath as well, Mikels remarked sarcastically, "Jeez … you could have at least texted or emailed me. I hate surprises!"

Vadim started to moan.

Mack observed, "We'll hogtie this one and store him in my van until we can get him to Rivera and his guys. How 'bout you get the kids and load 'em up. The driver knows the new destination, but he won't go until he sees your police identification. My New Jersey P.I. license isn't good enough for him."

Mikels laughed. "And Volkov just called me a man of action! You guys are too much." He turned away and stopped. "But what about Angel? We can't leave her here now."

"Bring her along too. She can handle the children better than we can. What are you gonna do?"

Mikels said, "I'll call Worten and see what he wants. In ninety minutes, this bus is gonna be late in a small town upstate. Volkov will realize something's gone wrong. He'll call Vadim's cell phone. Oh yeah, get the note in Vadim's pocket. The feds might be interested in Volkov's upstate contact."

Mikels took the steps at the East 10th house two at a time. Camila met him at the door with a surprised look. She said, "I didn't expect you here, Lieutenant."

Mikels thought, *There it is again. Disrespect!* He took Camila by the arm and pushed her down the hall, yelling loudly for Angel.

Angel came forward from the kitchen area with Alicia in tow. Seeing Mikels and the intense look on his face, she responded, "I'm here. What is it?"

Mikels, slightly out of breath from the stairs and man-handling Camila, said, "Get the kids. We're getting out of here."

Angel turned to Alicia with wide eyes, exclaiming, "We're getting out of here. Hurry!" She instructed Alicia to line up the children in the hallway. Both Mikels and Angel turned their attention to Camila.

Mikels said, "Now for you. You and your boss have been had. This game is over. You will shortly be arrested by the Brooklyn DA's office for child sex trafficking. Put your hands behind your back, sister."

With Camila in tears and handcuffed, Mikels called Worten. "Chief, things popped here beyond our control." Mikels explained the sudden turn of events and requested that Rivera meet him at Spasibo to arrest Arkady and Annika.

"Fantastic," said Worten, "your timing is perfect. I just hung up with the Brooklyn DA. He reported that the grand jury indicted everyone involved. Arrest warrants are being drawn up for Volkov, Arkady, Annika, the twins, and Camila as we speak. As long as you are aware of their existence, you don't need them in hand to make the arrests. Go for it!"

"We have Camila and Vadim, Chief. You might want to let the feds in on this now. We also have a Volkov contact in upstate New York they might find interesting."

After a brief and emotional meeting with Caleb, Angel guided the children onto the bus. With the bus running and ready to leave, Caleb leaned out from the door well and yelled, "C'mon, Jelly, let's go!"

Angel cupped her hands and hollered, "See you in Pennsylvania soon! Take special care of Alicia. I have something more to do." She blew him a kiss and ran back into East 10th. Caleb watched her charge up the steps. He thought, *I can't believe this ... they're right about her. What a woman!*

Mikels and Mack were talking in the hallway when Angel appeared and announced, "I'm going with you to Brooklyn. I want in on the arrest of those two."

They hesitated. She glared at the two of them. "And no freaking arguments from you two."

CHAPTER 50

A PLAN EMERGED. First, Rivera and his investigators would meet with Mikels, Mack, and Angel at Spasibo and take down the siblings. Then they would all go to Brighton Beach and arrest Volkov. If the FBI could get there on time, fine … if not, fine too.

Mikels and Angel walked along Clarkson Avenue while Rivera and his team prepared themselves on the next block. Angel paused at the alley and looked up at her fire escape. She smiled, picked up her stride, and said, "Let's do this."

Mikels caught up with her at Spasibo's front steps and grabbed her sleeve. "Whoa, little lady. Don't you think we should wait for the cavalry?"

Ignoring him, she pushed open the entrance door and said, "Nope. I earned this. Let's go."

Arkady heard someone stomping down the hall. He shouted, "Vadim, is that you?"

Receiving no immediate response, he went out into the hallway near Annika's office. He said quizzically, "What are you two doing here? Looking to get your old jobs back?"

Curiosity getting the better of her, Annika followed and approached Mikels, saying acidly, "Well, well, if it isn't the *Lieutenant*. I see you brought blondie along. What happened, Angel? Did Pappy Volkov get bored with you already?"

Angel turned to Mikels and asked, "Should I?"

Mikels nodded slowly and said, "Oh, absolutely!"

Angel grabbed Annika's blouse, yanked her forward with her left hand, and punched her as hard as she could with her right. Flat on her back with her nose broken and spewing blood, Annika looked up in shock.

Angel leaned over and calmly said, "Told ya I'd getcha, bitch!"

Mikels put his left hand up in front of Arkady's face, signaling him to stand still. He spoke into the Motorola two-way radio, saying, "Investigator Rivera, you may come in now and place these dirtbags under arrest."

Arkady's face paled. He spun around and ran down the hall to his office, and pulled open his center desk drawer. In panic mode, he charged forward with a small automatic pistol pointed at Mikels.

Mikels ducked, instinctively reaching for his weapon. But before he could pull it out, the narrow hallway reverberated with the deafening report of a single gunshot. Everyone froze.

Arkady staggered and collapsed against the wall, clutching his right shoulder. Looking back, Mikels saw Mack still pointing Eric Sullivan's shiny .38 caliber Chief's Special in Arkady's direction, smoke wafting from its two-inch barrel.

Mack swore. "Goddamn two-inchers. Never do shoot straight."

Mikels stood upright, took a deep breath, and sighed, "Straight enough … straight enough, Mack."

Greg Mikels—never again Gregor Mikhailovich—walked up to a demoralized Arkady and got in his paled face. He waved a hand melodramatically in front of Arkady's eyes, and with a contrived painful expression, whispered, "Poof!"

As tensions relaxed, Mikels's iPhone buzzed.

"It's Volkov. Should I answer it?"

Mack said, "Nah. Let him cook. Anyway, Worten said the feds were on their way over there. They should be arriving any minute."

Investigator Rivera read the two deflated siblings their rights and carted them off to jail, along with still unconscious Vadim retrieved from Mack's van. .

Volkov replaced the pool cue and called for his steward. He asked if any calls had come in for him.

"No, sir. The phone has been quiet."

He thought, *I can understand that nitwit Vadim forgetting to call, but not Gregor. I'll give it another half hour.*

He tried to reach Camila or Angel at East 10th but, again, got no answer. Concerned, he was about to call for his car to take him there when Ilia barged into the study unannounced.

Out of breath, the twin stammered, "Problems, boss."

Volkov stiffened. "What?"

"Something is going on over at East 10th. You told us not to get involved without checking with you, so I'm here."

Exasperated, Volkov demanded, "What do you mean? Explain yourself."

"I just saw Vadim getting onto the bus with Mikels. It looked like there was a struggle. Everybody was running around in a panic, and then the kids were loaded up. I tried calling Vadim, but he didn't answer. I'm tellin' ya, something is wrong. And shouldn't that bus have left for upstate a long time ago?"

Volkov began putting it together. Shock sapping his strength, he leaned against the pool table. He felt things unraveling. No call from upstate, no answer when he tried to call Camila ... and a struggle on the bus? Ilia wasn't the brightest bulb on the shelf, but he would know a struggle when he saw one. *This can't be happening!*

"Quickly ... let's go check with Camila."

Volkov pushed Ilia's back to move him along. "Go! Go!" They ran to Ilia's van and sped off in the direction of East 10th.

It only took a few minutes for Volkov to realize something was very wrong. Both buildings and the fenced yard between were empty.

He stood on the front porch with his hands on his hips. He spoke out loud, "Where are Camila and Angel? They wouldn't just leave." He felt a chill run down his spine. "Gregor ... I must call Gregor."

When Mikels failed to answer, Volkov tried Arkady and got the same result. He knew. There had been a major betrayal, and someone would pay. Not now. This is not the time for retribution. *First, I must get away.*

"Ilia, drive to the marina … quickly. You prepare *Bolshoi Babe* while I make some more calls."

FBI Agent Walt Jenkins strolled through Volkov's study with Chief Worten while agents combed the rest of the mansion. He stopped and leaned against the pool table, rolling a cue ball in his hand. He said, "We must have just missed him. The servants said he left in a van with Ilia about fifteen minutes ago. That's okay. He won't get far. We have all the bridges and tunnels under surveillance, and local cameras are being reviewed as we speak."

Chief Worten wasn't so sure. "I dunno, Jenkins. This guy's a slippery sonovabitch. I can't believe he doesn't have an escape plan."

Confident of his dragnet operation, Agent Jenkins shrugged off Worten's comment and changed the subject. "If those tapes are as you describe, the bureau has some work ahead of it. If indeed Volkov was in direct contact with Putin, there is an upstate spy cell we need to check out. In the meantime, I under-stand Senator Sturbridge is spilling his guts to the DA's office." He snickered. "That will shake up a few highflyers." He shook his head, smiling, and added, "You guys have jabbed a big stick in a hornet's nest."

Worten said, "I hope so. The only thing that keeps any business going—legal or illegal—is customers. Without them, there'd be no Spasibo or Volkov." He drove home his point further. "In my opinion, they're worse than the criminals that supply them with these kids."

Jenkins agreed. "Yeah, it's simple. It's like any commercial enterprise: supply and demand. If we could capture all the child predators, there'd be no need for traffickers."

Worten said, "I know, but an old police sergeant once told me, 'You can lock people up, but you can't legislate their morals.'"

"Yeah, pedophilia will be with us as long as man walks the earth. The thing is, we have to keep shoveling against the tide. That's our part in this mess we call law enforcement."

"I get all that idealistic crap, but right now we have more pressing demands: What about those who grab these kids in South America and bring them north? Who will go after them? Does anyone care? Will the bureau look into that too?"

Jenkins cleared his throat. "I wonder if Investigator Rivera could be attached to a joint task force to help on that end. Do you think his DA will release him?"

Worten replied, "That's a great idea. I'll put it to him."

Jenkins asked, "By the way, what did happen to those kids … the ones on the bus? Where are they?"

"Uh, we're working on that. At the moment, all I can say is they're with our people and they're safe."

Jenkins said, "We got a bunch of Asian kids at Spasibo too. Boy, did that little Filipina woman put up a fight! Two of our agents are nursing bruises."

Worten joked, "Serves them right. Shame on you guys, picking on a ninety-pound old lady."

Ignoring the gibe, Jenkins went on, "The government will be seizing all Spasibo's and Volkov's accounts, automobiles, and any other possessions that were part of their criminal enterprise. That includes this house and the two on East 9th and 10th. For your information, once we get this all sorted out, there will be a reward for any civilians who facilitated the investigation and assisted in the convictions of those we arrested."

Worten thought, *I know several who will be glad to hear that!*

CHAPTER 51

The bus arrives in Pennsylvania.

GRIPPING AN UPRIGHT post and leaning forward into the bus driver's well, Caleb recognized Eric Sullivan's pickup truck parked in front of 507 Country Store near Paupack.

Competing with the raucous din of twenty-four restless children, he tapped the bus driver's shoulder and shouted, "There … near the pickup!" Then he thought, *Jeez, the truck's right in the same spot I took off with it!*

Eric Sullivan eased himself off the rusty tailgate and limped toward the slowing bus, its hydraulic braking system hissing in protest. Caleb stepped down, wondering how this reunion would play itself out. He and Eric stood eyeing each other for a long moment.

Sullivan broke into a disdainful smile, saying, "Well, the prodigal truck thief returns." He stuck out his hand.

Caleb shook it rapidly. He tried to speak. "Sorry man, I had to— "

"Forget it."

Never short on sarcasm, Caleb said, "Hmm, 'forget it' … does this mean you forgive me too?"

"Don't push your luck, kid. I hear Mack has my damn gun. And please don't tell me you shot somebody with it."

Caleb went over the details of how Eric's little .38 Special won another gunfight with the bad guys which scored more points with the old man.

Eric laughed and quipped, "And they call it a 'backup piece.' Hell, that little gun ain't no way in second place."

Caleb got back on the bus and directed the driver to follow Eric to the summer camp four miles farther into the lake area.

Latitude 38°19'34.73" N, Longitude 74°54'56.27" W

Ilia manned the controls, keeping the sixty-one feet of *Bolshoi Babe* on a southerly course, gliding gracefully through mild Atlantic swells. They had made it undiscovered to just off the coast of Ocean City, Maryland. Volkov calculated that, between the two of them, they could maintain night-time operation of the yacht for five days—the time it would take to reach Cuba. During daylight, they would hide out in remote inlets and small marinas along the coast. The Sundancer's 2,102 horsepower dual engines hummed below decks, affording Volkov increased confidence every passing hour. His main challenge would be refueling. Their 930 gallons of diesel fuel were dwindling with every turn of the dual propellers. Ilia argued for slowing to preserve fuel, but Volkov would have none of that.

"Full speed ahead, Ilia. We are racing the clock before the FBI discovers we left by sea and sends the US Coast Guard for us."

He'd already figured they'd need three or four stops for diesel fuel, so he made calls ahead to Russian operatives along the East Coast to lend a hand in his escape. He'd rooted around in one of the boat's many lockers and found a banner that suited his purpose perfectly. Covering the words Bolshoi Babe painted on the stern, Volkov used Velcro to affix a shiny canvas he had made for just this purpose. It said, "Yankee Dream." He said aloud, "That should mess up their search a little."

Surrounded by the yacht's luxury, and with Ilia taking his turn at the helm, Volkov rested in the salon with a glass of Remy. He thought, *I may be gone, but I won't be forgotten.* He checked his Rolex. *Right about now, all hell is breaking loose back there.*

CHAPTER 52

TWO U.S. MARSHALS escorted a nervous Senator Maxwell Sturbridge from his apartment complex—one at each elbow. Looking around cautiously, they walked him from the entrance toward a waiting van with a marked police car parked at its front. All seemed securely under control.

Sturbridge asked the marshal on his right, "Is all this security necessary?"

Stern-faced and alert, the marshal answered disdainfully, "If I had my way, pal, you'd be on your own. Keep moving!"

A block away, waiting for just the right moment, Boris Krashenko peered through a pair of Russian BPOC 10x42 military field binoculars. Leaning forward and close to the van's one-way window, he said, "I told you they would park as close to the building as possible, Anatoly. It's protocol. To beat them, you have to play their game."

When the van side door slid open, revealing another marshal reaching out to help Sturbridge, Krashenko pressed the red button on a hand-held device. The electronic signal did its job perfectly.

Blasting upward from a storm drain a mere dozen feet from the rear of the marshals' van, metal particles mixed with stones and pavement fanned out in all directions, hurtling at over twenty-thousand feet per second. Sturbridge and the two marshals were killed instantaneously, their mangled remains scattered in a thirty to fifty feet semi-circle. The remaining marshal and uniformed officers were luckier. Their injuries were not life-threatening, even though their vehicles were shredded.

Boris the Bomb Maker calmly turned to his nephew, Anatoly, and said, "Ah yes—TNT, short for Trinitrotoluene—my favorite. It's messy but effective, don't you think? Let's go and scout out the next one."

Anatoly swallowed hard and drove off, saying, "Very messy, Uncle."

The federal building at 225 Cadman Plaza East, Brooklyn, New York was abuzz with the attack's aftermath. And Chief Worten was furious.

"How could this happen? Don't you people take proper precautions? A storm drain ... right under your noses, for Chrissake!"

The conference room held representatives from federal, two state, and three county law enforcement agencies. Mack counted nineteen in attendance—all sharing the same somber mood.

Responding to Worten's outburst, U.S. Marshal Chief Ralph Nixon said, "There's no call for recriminations, Chief Worten. We're all in this together. The question is, what do we do now? We have over twenty defendants to protect, and likely more coming as the FBI's investigation progresses."

Worten wouldn't be silenced. "Protection details are just that: you reconnoiter. You anticipate. You protect, and you do not take anything for granted." He bellowed, "Not even a goddamn storm drain!" He shook his head, disgusted.

Silence in the room echoed Worten's sentiments. It should not have happened. Members of the U.S. Marshal Service were experts charged with executing the Witness Protection Program nationwide. This was a serious breach of protocol.

But Chief Nixon's concern was valid too. He continued, "We must react in a coordinated fashion. As of this moment, everyone in this room is part of a new task force. We must not, and will not, allow the rule of law to be subverted this way."

Nixon went on expressing his indignation—as bureaucrats are prone to do—but without any immediate concrete recommendations.

On his way back to Elizabeth, Worten reflected, *He's been pushing papers too long. Another federal task force. Really? He needs to get out on the street and refresh reality!*

When Worten returned to his office, he gathered his own team together for a head-scratching session. Present were Greg Mikels, "Mack" Mackey, Bob Higgins, Linden Police Chief Andy Collins, and several members of the Union County Prosecutor's investigation staff.

Worten started by bringing everyone up to date. "I also just learned that a Wall Street banker and customer of Spasibo—meaning he was a child sex predator—was shot and killed by a high-powered rifle as he left his office earlier today. Naturally, no one saw anything, and the perp got away."

He waited for the group's murmur to die down before continuing. "Let's hope the feds get their act together and start protecting these witnesses before our whole case goes away. We need to concentrate on Volkov. I warned Agent Jenkins that

Russian was a slippery bastard. Can you believe our federal bureaucracy can't find him after just a fifteen-minute head start?"

Mack remarked, "I know they monitored every bridge and tunnel, as well as hundreds of surveillance cameras. The last I heard, they found Ilia's van dumped along the Shore Parkway."

Mikels offered, "I wonder if they followed up on that and researched possible Russian contacts Volkov might have in that area."

Worten ridiculed, "Who knows? That takes shoe leather. The feds not only move slowly, but they also don't share, and they sure as hell don't do tedious legwork. And they think they're smarter than everyone else."

Chief Collins chimed in confidently with, "Hey, Volkov's just another perp on the loose. It's not as if the guy can walk on water. He'll be caught sooner than later."

Bob Higgins bolted upright. "What did you say?"

Collins, taken aback, shrugged. "Huh? … Whaddaya mean?"

"You said he can't walk on water!" Bob searched the faces at the table and declared, "The sonovabitch has a boat! The reason no one has been able to pick him up is that we're looking in the wrong places." Bob nodded his head thoughtfully. "He gave us the slip by going out to sea."

Mikels said, "Oh my God! You're right. I remember him joking about my boat brochure and saying something like, 'That's not a yacht ... someday I'll show you a real one.'"

Mack said, "I'll check Coast Guard registrations for Volkov, but maybe someone oughta check and see if there's a marina in Brighton Beach and interview the dockmaster."

Mikels headed for the door and shouted over his shoulder, "Consider it done!"

CHAPTER 53

AFTER FOUR NIGHTS of taking turns at the yacht's wheel, Volkov and Ilia were tired. The weather had cooperated with calm seas, but the strain of avoiding capture had taken its toll. Las Olas Marina in Fort Lauderdale was loaded with vacationing tourists, all fawning over the yachts in the harbor.

Volkov cautioned, "Ilia, be sure to smile this time. Yesterday you were rude to the dockmaster in Jacksonville. People remember such things, and we don't want to be remembered. Now, pull over to the right. There's Viktor on the end of the second dock. See him waving?"

As Ilia deftly maneuvered the graceful Sundance to the refueling dock, Viktor Popov paced back and forth nervously. Once the yacht was tied securely and the diesel fuel began to flow, he joined Volkov onboard.

Doing his best to hide his growing apprehension, Volkov met Popov with open arms and a bear hug, as if this was a social call. Outwardly, Volkov was in control, but inside, his stomach churned. He surmised this meeting would tell him where he stood.

With his characteristic intensity, Volkov spouted, "Viktor Popov! We have not met since intelligence training. How are you enjoying life in the promised land?"

Popov, a diminutive man compared to Volkov and Ilia, was thin and stood at five feet seven. He wore dark-rimmed glasses and, with his pale skin, had the look of a bookkeeper. But Viktor Popov's reputation within the Russian spy system belied his physical appearance. He oversaw all Russian agents in the Southeastern United States and took his duties seriously. He was a loyal, Communist operative to the depths of his soul.

Returning the hug, he heartily slapped Volkov's back. With warmth gushing, he said, "Comrade Volkov, it is good to see you again. I wish it was under better circumstances."

Volkov poured a Remy for Popov as they settled down in the plush salon.

Popov got down to business. "I'm sure you want to know what has happened since you have been out of touch these past few days."

"Yes, of course, Viktor."

"Those you assigned to clean up certain problems have been doing well. The senator is gone, along with the investment banker. We are working on the rest, but enhanced protection details have slowed us down."

"What about the search for me? Any news there?"

"So far, so good. Nothing in our intelligence reports suggests that they know how you got away."

"We haven't reached freedom yet." Volkov sarcastically laughed. He added sarcastically, "If you consider an apartment in Havana freedom."

"I hear you, comrade. We have made arrangements directly with First Secretary Raúl Castro. He will look after your safety. I understand he has a new national identity prepared for you … Albanian, I think."

Volkov bowed his head and remarked, "Viktor, I am ashamed to say that I was taken in by a sexy woman and an undercover cop. I gave a lot of thought as to how this could have happened. I've had three days to think of nothing else. I know those two are responsible for this." He pounded his fist on a nearby bulkhead. "And I swear, they will pay."

Viktor Popov was expressionless. He thought, *I don't think so, Yuri Volkovitch.* But he commented, "Of course, my friend. There is time for that. For now, we need to get you gassed up and out of here. I arranged for a short-term slip near the end so you can catch up on sleep before heading out again tonight. Once you get going, you have only about six or seven hours to go before you are in Cuban waters. Then you can begin to relax."

"Yes. We want to time it so we approach Havana in daylight." Volkov paused, trying to come up with the right words. His voice subdued and anxious, he forced himself to say, "Viktor, I need to know where I stand with Vladimir on this. It's awkward for me, you know. Have you heard anything?"

Viktor looked straight into Volkov's eyes and lied, "No, nothing yet from headquarters. I will text you should he become involved. I'm sure he would understand. After all, you two have been friends for a lifetime."

"Hmm. True … but always in fair weather." He stared hard at Viktor, who held his non-committal expression, and said, "Viktor … you would tell me if I should be concerned. Yes?"

Viktor responded blandly, "Of course, Yuri. As far as I know, you have nothing to fear."

Ilia poked his head into the salon and announced, "All gassed up, boss. We have to get off the fuel dock. Others are waiting."

Viktor stood on the dock as Ilia slowly guided Bolshoi Babe —now labeled Yankee Dream—toward its temporary dockage. Yuri Volkov and Viktor Popov stood watching each other's images diminish as the distance increased.

Volkov thought, *I never could read you, Viktor. I wonder…*

Mikels walked across a short dock leading to the office of Marine Basin Marina at 1900 Shore Parkway, Brooklyn, New York. Inside, he was met by an officious young woman in her thirties who took her sweet time acknowledging his presence.

"Ahem. Could you help me, please?"

"Uh-huh." She continued busying herself by shuffling papers behind the counter.

Mikels waited until she looked up before speaking. "I have an important message for Mr. Volkov. I was told he was on his boat, but I couldn't find it. Could you direct me?"

The clerk went back to shuffling papers and said in a thick Brooklyn accent, "Not here. They left yesterday."

Bingo! Mikels maintained his composure and said, "Ouch! Did he say where he was going?"

"Nope. But they loaded up a shit-ton of supplies … and even paid for a full tank of diesel."

"'They?'"

"Yeah. He had a big guy with him … kinda cute in a rough way."

"Hmm. You make it sound like it's unusual to get a full tank."

299

"Almost a thousand gallons and all at once? Oh yeah. Not everybody does that."

Mikels turned to leave. He said, "Thanks for your help. Oh … one more thing. His boat is the big trawler, right?"

"No, he has a Sundancer 610. The biggest boat in the marina." She hesitated, frowned, and said, "Hey, I thought you knew him. You ain't getting nothin' more outta me, wise guy."

"That's okay. You did good, kiddo."

Mikels thought he'd just wander around the marina until he found somebody else. Scanning the boatyard as he walked, he noticed a black Chevy van backed in between two dry-stacked yachts. *Hmm, strange place to park. Probably nothing … just my cop brain working overtime.*

He approached a yard worker with, "Hey, how ya doin'?

The old man wore greasy overalls and a red ball cap. Before speaking, he sent a stream of tobacco juice off to his left. "Doin' okay, sonny. Ya look lost. Can I help ya with somethin'?"

"My wife and I were … she's over there on our boat." Mikels gestured over his shoulder. "Uh … we were trying to remember the cool name for that big Sundancer, the one the Russian owns."

"Oh yeah. It's 'Bolshoi Babe,' whatever that means. Nice boat, but the guy's a prick. A Ruski, ya know."

"Don't I know it? Thanks, pal."

When Mikels reached his car, he hesitated. He turned to face all the pretty boats posing provocatively just for him. He sighed, smiled wryly, and said, "Nah. It just wasn't meant to be."

CHAPTER 54

Aboard Bolshoi Babe—now Yankee Dream.

THEY GOT OFF to a late start. Volkov drank too much, and Ilia couldn't wake him at midnight as planned. Finally, just after dawn, they left Fort Lauderdale in their wake and set out for Cuba. By noon, the sun was hot but the breeze pleasant as they cut through the soft rollers below Key West.

At first, Volkov thought sadly, *I'll miss my American Dacha. It took me a long time to put all that together. But I knew there was always the chance something could go wrong ... which is why I planned for this day.* He relaxed, thinking about all the cash he'd deposited in the Cayman Islands. He grinned. *Enough to last five lifetimes.*

He held the wheel gently and shielded his eyes against the sun's rays by squinting, allowing out-of-focus colors to filter through. He could feel the Sundancer taking each caressing roll in its stride, swaying in concert with the ocean's choreography. He sensed oneness with the sea, the salty air, and the vastness of the sky.

His reverie was cut short. Off the port side, he spotted a small seabird skimming the wave tops, barely avoiding capture. He stiffened. Bitterness filled him. *Screw you, Batyushkov—you and your little birdie metaphor. Damn Dostoevsky! Damn you, Angel! God damn them all.*

Chief Worten had FBI Agent Jenkins on the phone. "Yes. We know where he is … that is, where we think he's going."

Skeptical, Jenkins said, "And what makes you think so?"

Ignoring Jenkins' cynicism, Worten continued, "Mikels did some poking around in local marinas and learned that Volkov and the second twin took off in a sixty-one-foot yacht named 'Bolshoi Babe.' They left yesterday with nearly a thousand gallons of gas and lots of supplies."

"Really? Uh … go on," said the FBI agent.

"Mack and Bob took to the phones and canvassed marinas all up and down the East Coast. It seems a Sundancer 610 is a very special boat … not many around, and people take notice of it. One has been gassing up at intervals between here and the Carolinas. No one remembers the name, but we think it's them."

Knocked from his superiority perch, Agent Jenkins was dumbfounded. "Jeez, you guys are way ahead of us. We've been shakin' up the Russians in Brighton Beach, figuring Volkov was hiding out there. Where do you think he's going?"

"Has to be Cuba. Where else?"

The Chevy van kept pace with Mikels but always stayed several cars behind. It swerved to avoid collision with a truck.

"Watch out, Anatoly. You're giving us away. Drive normally ... no jerky in-and-out stuff."

"Sorry, Uncle. The Belt Parkway always did scare me. You should be driving."

"Idiot! How can I drive and shoot at the same time?"

Mikels noticed a sudden movement to his rear. *What the hell. That's the van I saw in the marina.* He speed-dialed Worten. "Chief, I've got a tail on me. Could be I'm next on the hit list."

Worten sensed the urgency in Mikels's voice. He demanded, "Greg, where are you?"

"Belt Parkway, comin' up on the Verrazzano." He sped up to see what the Chevy would do. It passed several cars, keeping pace. "Oh yeah, Chief, I'm sure now."

"I'll call it in ... hang in there, Greg."

Mikels, nearing seventy-five miles per hour with his phone on speaker, yelled, "I'm getting off at Fort Hamilton. Call the military police at the main gate and tell them the good guy is in the white Ford Focus. Tell 'em to get ready for a shoot-out!"

CHAPTER 55

THE TWIN DIESEL engines hummed effortlessly below deck. Ilia busied himself with arranging lines and fenders on the foredeck while Volkov monitored their course at the wheel. A sudden movement off to the west caught Ilia's eye. It was another vessel … a fast-moving boat that seemed to be closing in on them. Soon, Ilia could see it was an ocean-going Cigarette boat, going so fast that it was airborne half the time.

Ilia stood up and saw that Volkov's eyes were fixed on the other vessel too. Ilia yelled, "Whaddaya make of it, boss?"

Volkov shrugged. He nudged the wheel westerly, an avoidance measure. The other boat countered with a matching turn. Volkov pulled back on the throttles. The Cigarette did the same.

Volkov hollered to Ilia, "It must be our Havana contact coming out to meet us."

Ilia nodded in agreement. But something troubled him. *Why don't they come right over?*

At that same moment, a U.S. Coast Guard MH-65 helicopter was flying its patrol grid at 3,000 feet over the Florida Straits, looking for drug smugglers. Captain Tina Wilson banked a hard left when she saw the tell-tale splashes of a go-fast boat in her windscreen. She spoke to her teammate via intercom. "Looks like we have one off the port side, Lou."

Master Chief Louis Bevans slid open his side door and followed the go-fast boat through binoculars. He transmitted, "Hey Cap, there's a slow-mover down there too. It looks like it could be a meet. Should I call for an intercept?"

"Let me drop down and take a closer look first."

The Cigarette boat slowed and came to a heading matching Bolshoi Babe but stayed a quarter-mile off Volkov's starboard side. As the go-fast boat pitched and rolled at a slow speed, two men were visibly eyeballing Volkov and Ilia through binoculars.

Volkov commented, "Hmm. That's odd. Why are they waiting? They're just looking at us."

In a sing-song voice, Ilia commented nervously, "I don't like it, Boss."

Volkov, from his higher perch, had a better view than Ilia. He saw one of the men duck below the other boat's gunwale for a second, then rise up with a long, barrel-like instrument and point it at Bolshoi Babe.

Realizing he had been set up, Colonel Yuri Volkov raised his face to the puffy clouds and waited helplessly. With eyes bulged wide, he screamed, "Putin, you fucking bastard!"

The missile spewed a trail of smoke, taking mere seconds to reach the hot twin exhausts of the luxury yacht. A millisecond after impact, the yacht's remaining gallons of diesel fuel ignited. The explosion was devastating. Shards of fiberglass, engine parts, cushions, exquisitely molded wood, and a half-empty bottle of Remy Martin XO rained down on the water's surface.

Master Chief Bevans yelled in disbelief, "Holy shit! Did you see that?"

"I'm calling it in now, Lou. Keep an eye on that go-fast."

"Will do, Cap."

The MH-60's purpose was to search and rescue, as well as drug surveillance. In this instance, however, it was apparent there wouldn't be anyone left to rescue. More importantly, the small helicopter was not intended for combat situations. Captain Wilson and Master Chief Bevans retreated to 6,000 feet above the water and waited.

Minutes later, Captain Wilson pressed on her left earpiece to better listen to air traffic over the helo's engine and rotors. "Hey, Lou, I just heard the cavalry is on its way."

A U.S. Navy F-16 fighter jet swooped low over the straits, homing in on the Cigarette boat. It was followed by a slower-moving U.S. Army AH-64 Apache helicopter. As the jet roared overhead, the go-fast boat crew unleashed a second missile. Alerted by a cockpit horn, the pilot of the F-16 released a unit of glittering aluminum chaff and banked a hard left.

Confused by the radiofrequency countermeasures, the missile homed in on the chaff and flew harmlessly out to sea until it ran out of fuel and dropped into the water miles away.

The pilot spoke into his headset. "Can you believe it? That little shit thought he'd shoot down a U.S. Navy fighter jet."

Following up, the Apache came in low. When the crew of the go-fast boat tried to reload their missile launcher, the Apache's side-door chain-gun opened fire as it screeched past at one hundred knots. Having accomplished its mission, the small, deadly chopper flew back to base, skimming indifferently over upstretched wave tops. This little sea bird had no interest in evoking romantic fantasy—it did its duty dispassionately and with precision.

Captain Wilson dropped her chopper down to near sea level to take a closer look. She reported back to base, "I see debris scattered all over. I count one, two … no … four bodies floating.

No sign of life. Hold it … the transom of the yacht is visible. Lou, can you read it?"

Viewing through binoculars, Master Chief Bevans spotted gold letters gleaming among the Sundancer's floating debris. "Yes, ma'am. All I can make out is Bolshoi … uh, something."

Wilson remarked dryly, "Well, that's one Russian who's had her last dance!"

Viktor Popov waited patiently. Overseas calls to Moscow took some time, especially to the Kremlin. Finally, he was put through. He recognized the voice immediately.

"Comrade Popov, give me good news."

"It's done, Mr. President. The Cubans did well, though they lost a crew to the Americans in the process."

"Collateral damage. Not a problem, considering what the Castros owe us. Well done, Popov!" He peremptorily hung up, and with a smirk, remarked, "Another one out of the way."

He strolled over to the heavy mauve drapes and leaned on the marble windowsill. Even at night, Red Square was clogged with traffic. He watched the headlights shimmering in the cold rain. He thought back several decades. *Ah, Yuri Volkovitch, we had good times, you and I. But this day had to come. You knew too much. You were a liability.* He stepped away and whispered matter-of-factly, "Poof!"

CHAPTER 56

THE CHEVY VAN was gaining on Mikels. A high-powered rifle slug shattered his rear window and penetrated the Ford's dashboard. Mikels took evasive action but swaying back and forth only slowed him down and allowed the van to close the gap.

Mikels screamed at Worten, "Chief, they're gaining on me … and I'm taking gunfire!"

"I have the MPs on the phone now. They're expecting you. Hang in there!"

Boris clutched the handgrip over the passenger door as his wide-eyed nephew held the pedal to the metal. "C'mon, Anatoly. I can't hit a damn thing with all this bouncing around. Get me closer!"

Anatoly shrieked, "I'm trying, Uncle!"

Boris pushed the rifle into the back and retrieved a Steyr tactical machine pistol with its thirty round 9-millimeter magazine from under the seat. "Get me close enough, and I'll pepper him with this!"

Mikels waited for the right moment and hoped his little car was up to what he had in mind. He waited until he passed the road leading to the Army's main gate and the van was close enough. In his rear-view mirror, he saw the passenger lean out and point a weapon at him.

"Now, little Focus, now!"

In one swift motion, Mikels threw the car into neutral, pulled hard on the emergency brake, and spun the steering wheel hard to the left. He drew his Glock and lowered his window as the small Ford—amid smoking and screeching tires—slowly revolved in a counter-clockwise direction and came to a jerking halt facing the oncoming van.

Just as Boris felt confidence in his shooting position rising, Anatoly instinctively slammed on the brakes to avoid hitting Mikels. Boris slammed head-first into the windshield and sprayed a dozen rounds harmlessly into the grass along the roadway.

"Damn you, Anatoly!"

Mikels accelerated. Driving close to the van's driver-side door, he let several wild shots off as he passed.

Anatoly screamed, "He's shooting at us!"

"Turn around, you idiot! Go after him." Boris wiped the blood from the gash above his eyebrow and punched Anatoly in the shoulder.

Mikels turned left into the main gate area with his hand pressed hard on the horn. The van started to follow but screeched to a jarring halt when Anatoly saw two armored Humvees strategically placed in front of the gate … along with a half-dozen uniformed military policemen with their weapons drawn. In the distance, police sirens could be heard approaching.

Boris narrowed his eyes as he took in the situation. "Okay, let's get out of here. Go back to Brighton Beach." Disgusted, he ordered, "Drive slow, and take side streets."

Chief Worten, still on speaker, hollered, "Christ, Mikels! What the hell is going on?"

"I'm a little shaky, but I'm okay, Chief. But someone is going to buy me a new back window and dashboard."

Mikels was coming off the Goethals Bridge into New Jersey when his iPhone rang again. Worten said, "Quick update: NYPD nailed your two buggers in the black van. As it happens, the SWAT team was returning from firing range practice and bagged them. Talk about being in the right place at the right time! When they saw SWAT deploy, they gave up like scared puppies. The sergeant in charge told me the old guy never stopped yelling at the kid all the way to jail."

CHAPTER 57

Courage, Forgiveness, and Redemption

MACK, BOB, MIKELS, and Angel piled out of Bob's van at the Pennsylvania campground. Caleb and Angel held each other in a long embrace. She gently ran her index finger along the scar on Caleb's head. No words were needed; their tears said it all. Angel felt a light tugging at her right elbow. She turned to find Alicia reaching up to her—more hugs and tears.

Caleb leaned over and said, "So you're what this was all about. It's nice to meet you, Alicia."

"Feliz para conocerte." She glanced up at Angel and said, "Umm, I mean, happy to meet you."

Angel proudly said, "We've been working on her English."

Later, Angel and Caleb strolled along one of the camp's wooded paths.

Caleb worked up the courage to say, "Jelly, I understand now why you stayed … the kids, I mean. But, uh, what happened to you there?"

Angel took a deep breath and reached for Caleb's hand. "Cal, do you remember when we first met? You saved me. You never pried. You never asked questions. It was so easy to lean on you, so I did. You tried to give me my life back, but I still wasn't right. Something was missing."

Caleb, his head down, kept walking in silence.

Angel continued, "Something happened to me that I still can't explain. When I learned those little kids were going to be sold for sex, it was like my brain exploded. In that second, I gave up feeling sorry for myself. Life was no longer just about me. It was about those kids. I couldn't stand by and watch them be pushed into the life I left—a life of shame, drugs, and all that went with it. I had no choice, Cal." She stopped and pulled Caleb around to face her. "I did what I had to do, and you have to understand."

Caleb chewed on his lip. In a hushed voice, he asked, "Jelly, is this one of those 'don't ask' moments?"

"It has to be, Cal. You need to know I love you and always will. But the world doesn't revolve around us. There are times for forgiveness. It heals the forgiver as well as the forgiven."

"Like a two-way street, huh?"

"Right," Angel sensed it was time to say it. "And you need to get your father off your back. The only way to do that is to forgive him. Hey, he had his life, and he lived it. He made his choices and mistakes like we all do. Don't let his mistakes ruin your life. Forgive him so you can move on!"

"You sound like Eric." Caleb kicked at a stone. "I don't know. Maybe you're both right. When I thought I lost you, I went crazy. I stole Eric's truck, and ... well, you know the rest. This has been a lesson for me too. I've been beating myself up, and for what? Nothing I can do will change what happened back then. My old man ... I guess I gotta get him outta my head."

On a lighter note, Caleb had more to say. "Did you know Mack offered me a job with his investigation company? He said I'm good on surveillance and I take great photos." Caleb blinked a couple of times and added, "He also told me that if I could dump the attitude I carry around, I might make something of myself."

"You know, he's right." After a short pause, Angel added, "One more thing: no more scammin'?"

Caleb laughed. "No more scammin', Jelly."

Angel leaned against a wide tree and gazed up at the sky. In a dreamy voice, she said, "For me, I'm gonna finish college and maybe even get a degree in child psychology. I'll help young girls escape from the sex trade. And I'm starting with Alicia. She has no family back in Honduras. I am—I mean—we are her family now. Mack says he'll help with her immigration status and see if we can be her sponsors. He said that the feds owe us that. He thinks maybe she can live with us too." She paused, letting the last part sink in before adding, "Cal, a long time ago, you proved to me you have a good soul. We need to do this together. Not for us, for Alicia."

"You mean, like a little sister?"

Angel took Cal's arm and started back up the path. She said, "Like a little sister … yeah."

Cal couldn't resist. "When we get back to Eric's place, I'll have to introduce you and Alicia to Big Louie."

"Big who?"

Caleb chuckled. "Big Louie. He runs the place. He's a kind of manager. He keeps everyone in line, especially the women in his life."

Angel's newly found feminism took the bait. "Oh yeah? We'll see about that."

Behind Angel's back, Caleb smiled ear-to-ear, and added, "I wouldn't ruffle his feathers if I were you."

Eric pulled up in his old truck, and Bob introduced him to Mack and Mikels. The four went inside the camp's main building to recap the events of the last ten days.

Mack sat back with his feet up on an empty chair. He broke open a Michelob and said, "Ya know, that Angel is one tough woman. She's got more guts than most men I know."

Mikels chimed in, "Tough and hard-headed, but with the courage of a momma lion. I wouldn't want to cross her." He thought a moment and said, "Actually, I did try, and it didn't work."

Bob said, "I owe you an apology, Greg. At first, I pegged you as a non-redeemable, crooked cop. But you've proved me wrong. What you and Angel did won't stop there. A big price tag is comin' down for some very bad people—some rich and famous bad people. You did good!" He shook Mikels's hand respectfully.

"Thanks, Bob. And I want you all to be the first to know that my chief promoted me to captain in charge of the Linden PD Detective Bureau. In a few years, my next stop could be Chief of Police. Not bad, huh?"

Dropping his boastful demeanor, Mikels lowered his head and paused. Embarrassed, he acknowledged, "I lost my way for a while. This case gave me my life back." Emotion welling up, he stopped talking and took a deep breath. Smiling gratefully, he not-so-artfully threw in, "Besides, a big boat is only a hole in the water you throw money into anyway, right?"

They all laughed.

Mack's cell phone rang. It was Chief Worten. Mack listened for a moment, then interrupted, "Chief, I'd like to put this on speaker for the guys here."

Worten said, "Just so you all know, there have been more developments. The photos of Volkov's calendar that Angel took have been translated. The feds are ecstatic. Volkov thought jotting in Russian was all the security he needed. His calendar gave up notes about meets with spies working in high tech companies, and—put together with what the FBI already knew—it completed the puzzle. In short, Angel uncovered a major Russian spy ring operating up and down the East Coast.

Also, Camila worked out a deal and gave up names and dates relating to child sex appointments set up by Spasibo and Volkov. Dozens of them. She even took the feds to a safe deposit box with stacks of money and videotapes of highflyers. It's all there wrapped up nice and tight. All I can say is, congratulations to you all. Well done!"

Mack paid for another round and sat back with a satisfied sigh, "Sometimes things just work out."

Mikels wistfully added, "We were lucky. It could have gone the other way."

Eric said, "I hate to break up this love fest, but do you have my little friend with you, Mack?"

"Oh, I almost forgot." Mack reached into his jacket pocket, retrieved the little revolver, and handed it over to Eric. But he couldn't resist a dig. "Damn thing doesn't shoot straight anyway."

Eric first made sure it wasn't loaded, then caressed the small revolver affectionately and said, "It shot straight enough to save my ass."

Mikels winked gratefully at Mack and mumbled, "Mine too."

Bob laughed and threw in his usual wise guy remark. "Yeah, that little gun works great for asses, but it doesn't do much for knees, does it, Eric?"

With his precious, shiny little sidearm pocketed, Eric turned and directed a caustic remark to Mack and Bob over his shoulder. "Hmph! What else would you expect coming from this Abbott and Costello team?" He limped off and muttered in mock disgust, "Ahhh ... I don't know."

In unison, Bob and Mack yelled after him, "Third base!"

The End (Or, should you prefer... poof!)

APPRECIATION

I WOULD BE remiss if I didn't express my thanks to those who encouraged, inspired, supported, and cajoled me to get this book done. Here are a few:

Albert "Doc" Bauman reads all my books. Nearly every time I see him, he says, "Hey, when is the new one coming out? You got me into reading again, and I need another one." Thanks for your constant "harassment" and your loyalty, Doc.

Thanks to Christine Wojick and her daughter, Sarah. Christine is one of several friends who volunteered to go over my first draft, checking the plot for tempo, continuity, and character integrity. I am also humbled that Sarah received an "A" for submitting her book report on *Loose Ends*, my first novel.

Judith White, a semi-retired educator/principal, provided much-needed insight and encouraged me to rethink parts of the plot.

Annmarie Gibson, our friend, and go-to emergency IT rescue person is always there when my laptop hates me. A simple thank you is not enough!

Brenda and Bob Higgins are real-life P.I.s in northern New Jersey and have always supported my writing efforts, as I do theirs. Again ... and again ... thank you, B&B, for agreeing to be characters in my novels. Happy fishing and have great book sales!

Lori Cirianni pointed out certain words in a sentence that had a double meaning and would have been embarrassing had they remained. Whew, close one! Good catch, Lori.

During evaluation sessions at The Middle Valley Writer's Group (New Jersey), I picked up lots of hints and shared some of my own. Special thanks to DJV Murphy and Charlie Levin, fellow group founders.

While researching child sex trafficking for this book, I came across several organizations meriting recognition and appreciation for what they do. Some agreed to interviews. Others encouraged me to quote from their websites. My deepest thanks go out to those who helped further my education into the dark shadows of human trafficking—especially child sex trafficking. After reading my book, if you would like to donate to organizations combating child sex trafficking, here are some worthy of your contributions:

Kim Checkeye, Director of Shelter Mentorship Program for The Samaritan Women-Institute for Shelter Care of Coopersburg, Pennsylvania spoke with me at length, adding to my education. She also turned me on to similar organizations fighting child sex trafficking. Her's is one of several sister organizations that cooperate with police and local prosecutors by operating stings to offer young women a way out of prostitution. To donate or inquire further, you are invited to visit https://instituteforsheltercare.org/give/.

In Bethlehem, Pennsylvania, Michelle Orr is vice president of Truth for Women and My Sister's Closet, an organization with a mission to help young women escape human/sex trafficking in Lehigh and Northampton Counties. Her husband, Matt, pointed me in that direction. Thanks Matt! Truth For Women offers a sanctuary for survivors of sex trafficking through its Truth Home, a haven for emergency stabilization. Through its twenty-four-hour care, Truth Home empowers women to heal and create a new future. Michelle Orr runs an upscale resale boutique that is the primary funding source for Truth Home. Donations are received through https://truthforwomen.org/.

UNITAS began combating human trafficking in 2015 after its founder, Lubo Krstajic, learned of the plight of trafficking victims. Believing in unity, as the name suggests, UNITAS quickly forged partnerships with governments, non-government organizations, and experts in the field to develop collaborative solutions in the fight against human trafficking of which child sex trafficking is a part. With offices in Belgrade, Serbia and New York City, UNITAS continues to advance innovative programs to expand regionally. They accept donations through their website: www.unitas.gov.

Another equally worthy organization is Stepping Stones in the Chicago area. Its mission is to educate and engage the community to prevent domestic, commercial sexual exploitation and to provide comprehensive, restorative care to survivors. Beginning in 2011, a group of concerned individuals in the northern suburbs of Chicago came together to discuss what could be done to address the growing problem of commercial sexual exploitation in the Chicago area. In 2014, they merged with Oasis Productions, and Stepping Stones Network was created. Stepping Stones Network is a program of Oasis Productions, a not-for-profit, 501c3 organization. Donations are tax-deductible and can be reached at: info@steppingstonesnetwork.org.

OTHER BOOKS BY DAVID BARTLE WATTS

―――――――――――――

ACCIDENTAL P.I.

A Private Investigator's Fifty-Year Search for the Facts
-A memoir by David Bartle Watts-

A real-life private investigator's memoir: his early experiences in law enforcement in the 1960s (including a race riot) as a young detective, right up to decades working on high-level cases for the Corporate 500. It's all here: fraud, theft, embezzlement, and murder ... and all true!

Attorney Robert Becker says:

An insider look at how cases are investigated and facts developed in preparation for trial, this memoir is also a candidly fun glimpse into the personalities and foibles of those involved. This is quality entertainment authored by someone who has "been there." A great read for those who appreciate authenticity.

Robert W. Becker, Esquire Civil Litigator in Albuquerque, New Mexico

———⁘———

Author Randy Wayne White says:

I thoroughly enjoyed Accidental P.I. by David B. Watts. It is a riveting series of tales that are all the more compelling because they are fact, not fiction, although Watts writes with the skill of a novelist.

Randy Wayne White is an award-winning, New York Times best-selling author of more than fifty books, including his popular *Doc Ford* Series. He is Florida's modern-day Hemingway—a literary legend.

LOOSE ENDS

Murder in the New Jersey Suburbs

-A Novel by David Bartle Watts-

What starts as a relatively low-level crime … insurance fraud … evolves quickly into a triple murder case in the up-scale community of Summit, New Jersey. A wealthy lawyer-turned-politician is charged with the brutal killing of his wife, while the real perpetrator goes on a killing spree to cover his crimes. The tension builds as the defense team cannot seem to get over its internal wrangling. An ambitious young assistant prosecutor steps over the line in her eagerness to convict the defendant. An unethical U.S. Congressman pulls the strings in the background, and all the while, the cunning killer, a psychopathic genius, does his share of devious meddling with the justice system.

Rob Whiteley, PhD and counseling
psychologist says:

Mr. Watts' long career as a private investigator and previous training in law enforcement provide a rich first-hand knowledge and foundation for creating a terrific read. He does a brilliant job of taking the reader behind the scenes, sharing a realistic view of the investigator's mindset and thoughts, while informing the reader about how the judicial scene can play out at the intersection of politics and the law.

There's nothing loose about "Loose Ends." The prose is tightly and intelligently written, and the plot or storyline is informative, entertaining, and enjoyable. The story is well-paced, and once I started reading, I could not put it down.

I am left waiting for this author's next novel. I hope that Mr. Watts uses his obvious and insightful experience as a long-time P.I. to craft a new adventure featuring this book's protagonist, "Mack" Mackey.

THE DEMENTIA CONSPIRACY
A Merger of the Corporate and Criminal Worlds
-A Novel by David Bartle Watts-

This gripping tale by a real-life private investigator melds the corporate and criminal worlds into one. When the push to beat the competition exceeds all reason—and with billions at stake—a pharmaceutical executive resorts to whatever it takes.

What do a hitman, a drug kingpin, a company vice president, a tainted clinical drug trial, three strong women, and a kidnapping have in common? Power, greed, revenge, and murder … of course!

Ex-SEAL and disgraced DEA agent Ted Archer is a mercenary who stops at nothing to achieve his goals. All pretense of decency aside, Archer wades through this story like a wrecking ball, killing, maiming, and destroying.

Reprising their roles in "Loose Ends"—Dave's first novel—Private Investigators "Mack" Mackey and Bob Higgins find themselves sandwiched between two sets of murderous criminals. Taking Archer and the others on, they are motivated by their sense of justice; yet restrained by their respect for the law. But their criminal counterparts have nothing holding them back as they arm up for the action-packed showdown. Replete with electronic eavesdropping, debugging, drones, and computer intrusion, this book has all a reader of thrillers could ask.

Author Dave Watts, a real-life private investigator, weaves another tale brimming with authentic investigative techniques familiar only to someone who has decades of being there. Don't start this one too late at night. You'll find it hard to put down.

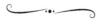

AUTHOR'S NOTE:

"Mark Twain said, 'Write what you know.' I do that. If you enjoyed 'Sex and Souls For Sale,' please write a review on Amazon ... and watch for my next book!"

Dave

ABOUT THE AUTHOR

DAVID B. WATTS, a licensed private investigator for the past four decades, specializes in fraud and business investigations. He and Linda, his wife of fifty-nine years, worked for major law firms, insurance companies, and the Fortune 500 in the busy New York to Philadelphia corridor on cases ranging from kickbacks to special security issues. He has also worked on several murder cases and thousands of insurance fraud matters.

Dave's investigation career began in his twenties as a Plainfield, New Jersey patrolman. He was promoted to detective, then joined the Union County Prosecutor's Office as a county investigator. These early experiences eventually launched him into a lifetime of investigation work in the private sector. His pursuit of the facts brought him into state and federal courts, as well as the board rooms of major corporations.

Authenticity comes through in his writing after a lifetime of experience, and he shares that with his readers. Who'd be better to portray the real ins and outs of private investigations in a novel? Go to Dave's website: www.davidbwatts.com for more information or to contact him.

CPSIA information can be obtained
at www.ICGtesting.com
Printed in the USA
JSHW032151050223
37281JS00002B/4

9 781662 844089